GNOME SWEET GNOME

ELVA BIRCH

For my readers.

You are a terrible, terrible influence.
Look what you made me not write!

LAWN ORNAMENT SHIFTERS

Short, hilarious, and full of heart, fall in love with the quirky
characters who run Wilson Kinetics, world famous artists
and lawn ornament manufacturers. Shifters meet their fated
mates in these clever, quick-paced stories of adventure and
romance, set in a world with shifters, gnomes, and more!

The Flamingo's Fated Mate (book 1)
Gnome Sweet Gnome (book 2)
Birdbath Bear (not that I'm writing it...)

CHAPTER 1

obias knew that people often wondered if he wasn't just joking about being a gnome because of his height. At five foot and no spare change, he was usually the shortest person in the room, and the shortest man by far.

He let them think that he was just saying it for a laugh, using the easy quips to break the ice and make sure that no one thought he took his own stature too seriously. He wasn't ashamed of his height, and he used other people's reactions to it as a measuring stick of character. Women who knew what they wanted would want him, and other men usually betrayed their own insecurities by realizing that he was everything that they wished they were.

But his gnome heritage was no joke at all, and that meant dutifully grooming every morning.

Tobias stared at his shaggy reflection. Every morning, his eyebrows needed to be clipped close to the skin. They looked thin when he was done with them in the morning, and by noon they were ordinary eyebrows. By evening, they were bushy and unkempt again. He usually maintained a beard, cutting a few inches off of it every morning, because it was easier than explaining why his five-o'clock shadow was a rug that few men could grow at all.

He kept his hair long, fine, and blonde like his Scandinavian ancestors, and trimmed it frequently to just past his shoulders. When he shaved it off altogether, he was barely bald for a day, sprouting to a buzzcut by that night. In a few days, he was scruffy, and in a week, he was in "get a job, hippy!" territory. He had grown it to his waist briefly in college, but it had been unruly at that length, so he preferred it somewhat tamed.

Fortunately, it was only the hair on his head that was so super-charged; the rest of his body had a decent dusting of curly hair, but it didn't tend to be quite so *take-over-the-world* as the follicles in his face.

There was a handsome face beneath the hair, Tobias knew, and sometimes he shaved clean just because he liked the effect it had on people of both sexes.

Today…Tobias fingered his beard. It was on the long side right now, and Frank had been making noises about having him play a Christmas elf at the rescheduled charity gala that evening.

"Now that it's so late in the year anyway, we should lean into the season," the flamingo shifter had said.

"Candy cane cupcakes!" his new mate, Anita, exclaimed in joy. "And gingerbread!"

Tobias liked Anita, in small doses. She was pretty intense and excitable, and Frank was absolutely swept away by her, going along with every crazy plan that she came up with. Fortunately, her interference seemed to be limited to refreshments, and Tobias was relieved that she seemed to have very little interest in Frank's business management or in his money at all.

Tobias told himself that he wasn't jealous. He was a gnome of the noblest lineage, fabulously wealthy, devastatingly handsome, and brilliant to boot. What did he care if his best friend had a new favorite person?

He'd known about shifter mates, but he hadn't really believed in them until he saw how Frank looked at Anita, like she was the other half of his soul. Tobias knew what infatuation was, and he was skilled in reading people; this wasn't empty attraction or passing fancy. Frank was head-over-heels for the curly-haired baker, absolutely smitten, to the bottom of his big, pink, flamingo heart.

Tobias didn't need that. He didn't want to be anchored to a single person like that, attached at the hip to just one woman. It wasn't like he was lonely or unfulfilled. He picked up the heavy-duty trimmer (he had a dozen of them, and went through them like most people went through flossers) and frowned at his reflection. This gala would attract the most important people in the city, and he was one of them. He had an image to maintain.

Sometimes, he feared that image was all that he had.

CHAPTER 2

Harriet surveyed the ballroom from the top of the stairs.

The last time she'd been here, the place had been silent and dark, without power and in the grips of a record-setting snowstorm that muffled it like cotton. The only other people in the whole building had been Anita, Harriet's bubbly rival baker, and Frank Wilson, philanthropist and flamingo shifter.

Harriet had been forced into hiding, trying to stay out of their sight but unable to avoid witnessing their awkward and over-the-top courtship. Could he take her up to the penthouse like a normal hot-blooded shifter with his mate in his sights? Oh no, they had to build a fort in the ballroom out of tables and curtains, giggling over games of pretend and elaborate drawn-out emotional square dances.

It was enough to make Harriet gag at the memory. An entire wasted day, with nothing to show for her trouble but a few flamingo bites and a bruised ego. She hadn't even had a chance to pry any jewels out of the fancy flamingo sculpture to make her trip worthwhile.

But the second time was definitely the charm and Harriet felt optimistic and energized. The table fort was gone, and this time, the space was warm with light and music...and marks. She just needed to stay out of the way of the hosts and fill her pockets.

Her owl was fluttering in her chest more actively than usual; did this bode well for her luck tonight? Certainly, the crowd that had turned out looked like they had more to prove than ever, decked in their holiday best. Nothing said *charity* like wearing a fortune in priceless jewels while they wrote magnanimous checks for a tiny fraction of their daily spending money.

Charity.

Harriet hated that word.

She hated everything that came with it. She hated the embarrassment of food bank boxes and the shame of hand-me-down clothes and the sting of carrying her earthly possessions in garbage bags because even *used* luggage was an unspeakable luxury.

Harriet smoothed the hair back from her face and forced herself to smile at a man who brushed against her at the top of the stairs. He wasn't expecting her sudden simper and practiced giggle and nearly pitched himself down the stairs when he missed a step, but Harriet was gone by the time he looked up again, melting into the crowd with practiced ease.

He was also lighter, by a very cheap watch. Harriet had assumed by his suit that it would be a decent fence, but she was disappointed by the brand and left it in a bowl of fruit when she made it down to the buffet, cataloging the guests by the table.

Buffets were child's play for lifting jewelry. It was so simple to reach for something at the same time, to jostle against someone, or spill some opportune food. Carelessly daubing at someone's glittery frock would catch everyone's attention and no one would even notice what she was doing with her other hand, with everyone close and concerned.

Pecking at the food offerings were the elite mix that Harriet expected at a charity gala. Senators, television anchors, minor celebrities, all of them desperate to impress each other and prove their generosity while eating tiny food off of toothpicks.

Well, Harriet was perfectly willing to help them with that *generosity.* All she had to do was avoid Anita and Frank, and rip off a few of their guests to settle her debt of honor.

Harriet's owl was hopping in her chest. *Who? Who? Who? Who?*

Her owl didn't usually care about who Harriet targeted and was generally disdainful of shiny material things, protesting that she was no raven. But this evening she seemed particularly tightly wound.

What has your feathers in a ruffle? Harriet asked.

Who? Who? Who?

Birdbrain. Harriet thought it fondly. She didn't know where she'd be without her owl companion. Lonelier, for sure, probably desperate enough to settle down with some useless guy just so that she didn't have to hear the silence in her own soul. Not that her owl was stimulating conversation, but it was better than a hollow emptiness that jewels couldn't fill.

She was also grateful for her shifter reflexes, especially when someone bumped into her as she surveyed the sugar-shimmering dessert selection.

Harriet knew deliberate bumps. She had *perfected* deliberate bumps and she was outraged that someone might try one on *her.*

She turned to give a scathing rip-down and her owl exploded in her head. *Him! Him! Him!*

CHAPTER 3

*T*obias had all but given up on the gala as a dead bore.

He'd been to a hundred of these things by now, and he mentally checked each guest off in his head. Senator Helen Gable. Victoria Hennings, the popular TV anchor. Real estate mogul Clara Bigges. A lot of important people with no real substance. Tobias was tired of shallow billionaires and grasping wannabes.

He'd rather be on the Wilson Kinetic factory floor than at this gala, working with Frank and Bruno on the next proto-type, or doing something with his hands. Something in bed with his hands would have been fine, but his search through the guests left him cold and uninterested. None of them had any depth. There was no *spark.*

Tobias told himself that it wasn't just that he was comparing them to Anita, to the way that Anita lit Frank up like nothing ever had before.

Anita would have driven him up an ever-loving wall. He didn't want her non-stop chatter or her bouncy, irrepressible energy. After a few hours of her presence, he needed a stiff drink and a roll of duct tape. She wasn't at all what he was looking for.

But she made him think that maybe there was something more out there than one-night stands and congenial arrangements for mutual satisfaction.

Something *real.*

And just when he'd decided that no one *real* would ever come to a social swap-meet like this, he saw her, standing at the buffet table in a tableau of perfection.

She was a shifter, by her lanky grace, or Tobias would eat the fake white beard that Frank had convinced him to wear over his shaved jaw. She was taller than he was, which didn't say much, and was wearing a sleek, shimmering gown of silver that would have looked overwhelming on anyone else. Coppery red hair was piled on top of her head in artful curls, exposing a long neck and strong, pale shoulders.

There was a velvet choker at her neck, and she wore no bracelets. But what Tobias noticed first about her was her keen *awareness.*

She was masterful at hiding her observation, he thought, with a practiced nonchalance in every line of her body, but Tobias was watching her when someone nearby fumbled their fork. She reacted nearly as fast as they did, and reined in her automatic motion just as quickly. If Tobias hadn't been studying her, he'd never have noticed her noticing, or her precise control.

He timed his approach when she was doing another surreptitious survey of the other people at the buffet, jostling her just a little as he reached for a cube of cheese on a tiny stick.

She turned to him with flashing golden-brown eyes, clearly not fooled by a move that he'd used to successfully break the ice with dozens of other women.

Because she was clearly not just another woman.

Tobias had experienced plenty of *moments*. He might not be a shifter, but he had his own brand of supernatural power, and he had strong instincts that never failed to steer him right. They'd led him into lucrative business partnerships and put him in the right place at the right time. He'd learned not to ignore that zing of certainty that told him when a chance encounter was something more than chance.

And that intuition was guiding him now, telling him that this woman, this gorgeous, graceful, self-contained goddess, was something more than just another gala guest.

"I'm Tobias," he introduced himself, flourishing the square of cheese at her. "Have you sampled the smoked gouda?" He forgot that he was wearing the ridiculous Santa Claus beard until he tried to grin winningly at her. Why *did* he let Frank talk him into wearing it? He was always a good sport about the short jokes and never took himself too seriously, but he caught himself wishing he'd gone with dignity over comic whimsy this once.

She didn't answer, frozen and staring at him as if he'd just spilled soup on her shoes and she was trying to figure out whether or not to hit him with her purse.

It was probably the beard.

"Ch-cheese?" she said faintly.

"A delicious dairy concoction served at the end of tiny wooden stakes," Tobias teased her. "Also a primary ingredient of nachos, one of life's small *pleasures*."

The use of the word pleasure was deliberate, and it always served Tobias well to remind people what he was offering them.

He greatly underestimated what it would do to this woman.

She flushed the kind of red that only natural red-heads could aspire to, despite Tobias's initial assessment that her hair color was from a bottle, and her hand, clutching a purse, actually trembled. Her lips parted slightly, and she licked them, then swallowed.

"Not many people use gouda on nachos, mind you," Tobias said, trying not to stare too obviously at her lips. "But it pairs beautifully with chicken, especially if it's smoked."

His attempt to eat the cube of cheese seductively for her was thwarted by the Santa beard. The frizzy fake hair didn't give him the same cues that his own follicles would.

She didn't seem bothered by the fact that he had to untangle his food from the poorly-constrained holiday costume. She did, however, continue to seem *bothered.* Her eyes were wide and bright, and her movements nervous.

"Ch-chicken nach-chos?"

Even stuttering, she had a sultry, silky voice; it wasn't like Anita's at all. Tobias thought that he actually would be happy to listen to her prattle about anything.

If he could coax more than a few words at a time out of her at all…"Are you bidding on the flamingo sculpture this evening?" he asked.

The woman made a visible effort to gather her wits, drawing in a deep, slow breath and clenching her hand at the handle of her purse. "I'm sure it's out of my price range," she said carefully. "I'm only here for…the *refreshments.*"

Tobias nearly offered to *be* one of her refreshments, but decided that he had already unsettled her enough. She was clearly not prepared for the kind of staggering effect he could have on people. Indeed, Tobias was surprised that his charms had been this potent; he thought he'd be at a disadvantage with the ridiculous Christmas gnome getup, but perhaps she had a fetish for fake beards and jingly holiday shoes.

Tobias could work with that.

CHAPTER 4

*H*arriet's saving grace was that she was pretty sure that Tobias didn't *know* that he was her mate.

As long as by *saving grace*, she meant *I have turned into a complete idiot and I can't stop imagining him naked.* Having an owl in her head who fluttered and cooed every time the infuriating man said a word was the worst thing that Harriet could imagine. But Tobias seemed no more than casually interested in her—attracted to her maybe, but he was clearly not battling back animal instincts like she was, unless he was a much better actor.

He might have been dressed as a Christmas elf, and at least a foot shorter than Harriet, but she had never been quite as bowled over as she was by this man. He was built like a bulldozer, with broad shoulders and a narrow waist in a tailored Christmas suit trimmed in gold embroidery.

He was also wearing a long white beard and sporting turned-up shoes with bells on them.

"This hall has beautiful artwork, don't you think?"

Was he trying to make small talk?

Harriet glanced up at the paintings above the buffet table. "Pre-revolutionary French salon art," she observed out of habit. "Not as good as Capet or Labille-Guiard."

"I don't know those artists," the man said frankly, instead of pretending he knew everything the way Harriet had expected. It was unnerving.

I stole one of their paintings from a museum, Harriet almost blurted. She was going to have to keep a close watch on her tongue under her owl's terrible, trusting influence.

"Have you tried the cupcakes?" he asked.

Harriet shot him a look of consternation, but the question appeared to be innocent. There was nothing to tie her to Patty Cakes, her bakery chain, or to Anita, or to any pastries at all. He was only offering her food.

"There's a spicy hot cinnamon," he added coaxingly.

Dangerous, *dangerous* food. And also, damn Anita for coming up with really interesting flavors. It was a brilliant idea.

"I'm on a diet," Harriet lied. Shifter metabolism kept her in fighting trim no matter what she chose to eat. But it was the kind of statement that discouraged offers of food. Oh, damn, she'd already told him that she was there for refreshments. She was going to look like an idiot.

Tobias, however, was not so easily discouraged. "There are carrots," he offered. "And celery. I'm not sure what those green things are."

We are not a rabbit, her owl said in outrage.

"It's a *meat* diet," Harriet said hastily, and when Tobias glanced at the table to see if there was anything not vegetative, cheese, or loaded in carbs, she gathered her skirt up in her hand and fled, darting behind some gossiping celebrities and making a beeline for the exit.

You're going the wrong waaaaaay! her owl wailed. *He's back there! He was going to* **feed** *us!*

Harriet had a feeling that accepting food from Tobias would have been a mistake equal to Persephone's. If she ate his food, from his fingers, she'd be lost forever, in some kind of sappy, lovesick hell.

Tobias would make a dashing lord of the underworld, she thought, as she elbowed her way through the crowd towards the event hall exit. She could actually picture him as Hades, like Tim Curry from *Legend*, all temptation and terrible judgment.

Unfortunately, that meant that she was now picturing him shirtless.

If she hadn't been on absolute fire before that image was burned into her brain, she certainly was now. It didn't matter that she hadn't gotten a good look at his face through the ridiculous beard he was wearing. His eyes were enough, dark green and heated, and Harriet could tell that he was well-built, stocky, and strong. He hadn't shown the slightest discomfort, having to look up at her; he had a sizzling self-confidence that was incredibly sexy. His hands had caught Harriet's attention, strong and nimble. She could imagine what he could *do* with those hands…

"Excuse me," she said impatiently, trying to dodge around a couple who somehow thought that the middle of the hallway was the perfect place for a lengthy conversation with a dozen people.

The curly-haired woman turned and exclaimed, "Harriet Slade!"

It was Anita, the world's most annoying baker, and the very last person that Harriet wanted to see. Her situational awareness had apparently gone out the window at the unexpected sight of her mate. "Anita," she said quellingly, trying to sidle past. Avoiding Anita and Frank had been basically her *only* criteria for the night.

But Anita was already bouncing towards her for a

chummy no-boundaries hug. "Oh, it's so nice to see you! I didn't realize you were on the guest list." Then she stepped back with alarm. "Oh, *are* you on the guest list? Are you here to sabotage my cupcakes?"

"Ha ha ha," Harriet said, glancing over their rapt audience and eyeing Frank, the host of the whole event and her second least favorite person at the moment. Frank eyed her skeptically back. Her effort to slip out unnoticed was being neatly thwarted and she glanced to see if Tobias had followed her, both glad and sorry to see that he hadn't.

"Oh, it's the funniest story…" Anita said, turning back to a bejeweled older couple that Harriet recognized as Councilwoman Henderson and her very wealthy husband. "Remember when the charity gala was first canceled because of that snowstorm? I hadn't gotten the notice, so there I was with two thousand cupcakes…"

At any other time, Harriet might have been interested in the antique diamond necklace and matching bracelets that the councilwoman was wearing, or the gold wristwatch that her husband was sporting. This would be the perfect opportunity to let Anita take the spotlight while Harriet leaned on them in feigned laughter to slip open their clasps and relieve them of a small fortune.

But she was too bothered by the memory of Tobias and the fathomless depths in his eyes when they'd locked gazes. He'd offered her *food*.

Her fingers were trembling too much to make a smooth snatch, and her owl was hooting in her head: *HIM HIM HIM HIM HIM.*

CHAPTER 5

Were the beard and the shoes too much after all? Tobias wondered, watching the woman flee athletically through the crowd.

He wasn't sure what to make of her. He was quite confident that their attraction was mutual, but he couldn't figure out what he'd done to scare her away so thoroughly. One of the major advantages to being short was not being threatening, but the beautiful stranger had acted as if he'd just pulled a knife on her, not offered her food from a buffet. Food was usually a safe subject.

He frowned down at a cheap watch that someone had lost in a bowl of fruit. He also didn't believe for a moment that she was on a meat diet.

Tobias took another thoughtful cube of cheese and then went in deliberate search of Frank to try to sniff out who she was. He told himself, walking politely through the crowd, pausing to laugh with friends over his ridiculous get-up, that she wasn't that big of a deal. She was just a puzzle, and that only made her seem more fascinating than she actually was. Tobias enjoyed solving mysteries.

The jolt of excitement in his chest when he caught sight of her glittery dress and red hair suggested that it was more than just the mystery of her that had caught him, but Tobias hung back, waiting and watching. She'd been caught in a conversational web and Anita was hanging onto her arm telling an enthusiastic story punctuated with broad gestures that threatened anyone in reach.

He could hear just enough of Anita's tale to know that it was about the fateful day that she'd met Frank, trapped by a snowstorm in this very hall without power. He'd heard the saga several times now, including the unvarnished version that involved Harriet Slade, Anita's baker rival.

Harriet Slade.

Tobias tasted the name in his mouth. That had to be her, judging by the gesturing and laughter, and the way Anita was hanging on her arm and gesturing to her.

Harriet was an owl shifter, which explained her grace and strength, and she and Frank had engaged, by all accounts, in a very dramatic aerial battle when he caught her lurking in the event hall where they'd been trapped.

Tobias privately suspected that there was something missing from Harriet's explanation that she had snuck into the event hall early to sabotage Anita's cupcakes. He liked Anita, but felt that she was terrifically naive, and Frank wasn't much better. Tobias wouldn't have fallen for such a story.

He eyed the woman, assessing the height of her heels, the style of her hair, and her accessories. She wore a necklace—and a nice one!—with matching earrings, but no rings or bracelets. The dress was not off the rack; it was either couture, or custom. It was designed to pull attention away from Harriet's face, like her bright hair. People would remember the dress, the scarlet locks, and the daring cleavage, not the woman.

Well, other people. It was her face that Tobias recalled best, her golden-brown eyes flashing and her mouth in a little O of surprise. There was something about her, about the planes of her cheeks and the tilt of her jaw that seemed to resonate with him.

He returned his gaze to the dress, eying the lines down her back. It was a lot of dress for a baker, even the owner of a chain of successful bakeries. Tobias knew a lot about profit margins in a range of fields and he was dubious that Harriet had the scale of economy to get a return that would pay for the lifestyle she was clearly pulling off—Anita had already commented on her "very nice car." Tobias suddenly wondered jealously if she had someone paying for these things in return for personal favors, surprised by his own fierce reaction to the idea.

This Harriet woman really had gotten under his skin and Tobias reminded himself that it was just as likely she'd come from money as that she had a generous boyfriend. He wasn't the possessive or jealous type, and he had no reason to get all bristly over a woman that he'd just met.

He just liked a challenge, he assured himself.

And Harriet Slade was definitely going to be a *challenge*.

CHAPTER 6

*H*arriet was surprised that Anita's story, frivolously embellished, painted her in the flattering light that it did. The curly-haired baker made Harriet's planned sabotage of the cupcakes sound like a friendly prank, not a catty business move or a petty act of malevolence, inviting her audience to enjoy it without judgment. She kept both Frank and Harriet's shifter identities secret, and spun the day as a wholesome slapstick comedy of errors.

Hard as she tried, Harriet could not find an opportunity to slip away; Anita clung to her arm like a chummy leech and they had the focus of everyone around them.

"Our table fort was just there," Anita said, pointing. "I wasn't going to let Frank take me up the penthouse five minutes after we'd met, that's the kind of thing a man's got to earn, and he'd just spent so long convincing me that he was a janitor."

"Fortunately," Frank said with an adoring laugh, "I've since earned those penthouse permissions…"

Everyone laughed and they exchanged a kiss that Harriet hoped would finally be her chance to escape.

Unfortunately, Anita didn't actually *let go* of her. Frank glanced up as their kiss—Harriet as a reluctant third wheel—finally broke off.

He was looking beyond her. "Oh, Tobias, is it time for the auction?"

Even his name made Harriet feel weak-kneed and she knew before she turned who was behind her. It had taken her an embarrassingly long time to get past her ridiculous reaction to him and realize exactly who he was.

Tobias Underhill was generally agreed to be the brains behind Frank's fabulous success as a lawn ornament artist. He was the flamingo shifter's business manager, a man of considerable financial success of his own. Major publications estimated his wealth in the billions, and he was often shown on glossy magazine covers with supermodels and actresses on his finely-shaped arms.

Harriet had always considered him not at all her type, but conceded that he was handsome enough if you liked short, successful playboys. He had a dashing smile and a confident gaze, thick blond hair that was long, for a man, and of course, lots and lots of money.

He was also very bold about claiming to be of noble gnome heritage, which was the sort of thing that was met with disbelieving laughter and tolerant nods.

No one was really sure if he was serious. Though shifters were known and generally accepted since they'd come out of hiding, gnomes still seemed a little far fetched.

Gnome or not, Harriet was stunned and appalled by her reaction to his proximity. Was it only chance that they had not run across each other any sooner at art auctions or museum fundraisers?

Or was it destiny?

Maybe it was because Harriet generally eschewed *charity*

events, preferring to hit exhibitions that didn't try to varnish greed with hollow philanthropy.

To her mixed relief and utter annoyance, Tobias completely ignored her. "It's time for the unveiling," he said, grinning through his ridiculous fake beard at Anita and Frank. "If I could steal your fiancé for a moment, Anita?"

Anita gave Frank one final kiss, kicking up her leg and posing dramatically to audience giggles. Then she let Tobias lead him away through the crowd, the two of them pausing frequently to make inane small talk with the other guests.

Anita still hadn't let go of Harriet. "You'll keep me company during the auction, I hope?" she begged quietly near Harriet's ear. "We bakers have to stick together and everyone here is so *fancy* and important. Senators keep trying to make friends with me so that Frank will do commission work for them. Apparently everyone knows that I'm a pushover, and that Frank is a pushover for me, but I don't want him to have to do a sculpture because I can't say no."

Harriet was still too shaken by the sight of her mate to pry Anita's fingers off and get away without making a scene, and besides, she felt a little sorry for Anita, who had clearly been thrust into a class of people she was poorly prepared to handle. She also worried that she technically owed Anita a debt for her kind treatment in what could have been an awful story after she'd been nothing but unfriendly.

And Harriet always paid her debts.

"Sure, sugar queen."

Then Tobias took the stage.

He held a glass aloft and tapped on it with a fingernail until the hall fell quiet with a wave of people shushing each other.

"I'd like to thank you all for coming out tonight to spend a lot of money for a very good cause. As you all know, the charity chosen by Wilson Kinetic this year was the flamingo habitat fund, and there's a bit of a funny story behind our choice. As a company based in lawn decoration, we have never before had a flamingo in our line."

A few people chuckled and there was a murmur of speculation.

"Frank agreed that this was a drastic oversight, and his sculpture for this year's line, I think you will agree, was absolutely…inspired."

The speculation turned to suspicion.

"Here to present this year's Wilson Kinetic designs is the artist himself, Frank Wilson!"

Tobias started a round of applause that propelled Frank up onto the stage and Anita finally let go of Harriet in order to clap and whistle and cheer.

Harriet knew that she was supposed to be watching the reveal of the ridiculous flamingo sculptures, but she'd already seen them, and wound them up herself, and Frank, giving his own short pre-reveal speech, could not hold a candle to Tobias's sheer magnetic personality.

It was astonishing how Tobias could have twice the presence as Frank, who was supposed to be the celebrity of the evening but seemed like a quiet, colorless clod by comparison. And damn, Tobias could even look handsome wearing shoes that turned up at the point and were hung with bells.

Harriet shook herself, realizing that she was staring at him. This was her chance to get out of here unnoticed, and she was going to blow it drooling over the master of ceremonies like a complete rookie.

The audience was tight with anticipation and Tobias read the room perfectly and signaled Frank at just the right moment to yank off the sheet obscuring the kinetic statue.

The sheet-snatching motion was embellished with a swell of music and lights that lit the monstrous thing up like a carnival ride, illuminating gleaming pink diamonds and rubies and garnets and opals.

Frank gave them a moment to drink in the bejeweled figure, then gave a crank a few turns to put the mechanical portion into motion. A few strong twists, and the thing was dancing in place.

Harriet wasn't that impressed by the stationary aesthetics of the sculpture, though she was dispassionately sure that it had a small fortune in jewels encrusted on it. Pink was not her favorite color and flamingos were more absurd than art to her. But she could not deny the grace and balance of the mechanism of the statue, or the fluid way that it moved. It was a work of genius.

The crowd cheered but Harriet was looking at Tobias again, trying to decide what his expression was behind that awful beard. He was watching Frank, looking as pleased and proud as if he'd made the sculpture himself. Then he swung his gaze out over the audience and caught sight of Harriet.

This time, he didn't pretend that she didn't exist, staring right back at her over the heads of the millionaires of the city and straight into her soul. Her owl hopped in place, unbearably excited.

Dammit, Anita was clutching at her again, closing her window of opportunity to escape. Her cover was blown, and this whole evening had been one frustration after another.

The reveal continued to the prototype of the smaller, plainer version of the flamingo that would be available affordably to homeowners everywhere and Tobias kept his eyes on Harriet while Frank demonstrated its mechanics.

It was a cliched gaze across a crowded room, except that he was standing on a stage and Harriet was draped in excited, clingy baker…and she could not drag her eyes away from him for any reason.

He was the one who looked away first, and Harriet cursed her weakness when it felt like she'd lost something.

"We will begin the bidding at one hundred thousand dollars," Tobias called. "You could be the proud owner of this cunning mechanical wonder for a low, low opening bid…"

Several dozen paddles shot up into the air and Harriet watched in wonder as Tobias played the crowd like a musical instrument, coaxing higher and higher bids out of them, teasing and quick-witted. He seemed to recognize all of the bidders, calling them out by name, referencing little bits of their history, and Harriet was frankly impressed and a little turned on.

Someday, Harriet thought, fanning herself, she would have to coordinate a heist of one of Frank Wilson's coveted art sculptures. Wouldn't it be fun to watch them reveal nothing at all? It would take incredible coordination and it probably wasn't something she could do herself; the flamingo probably weighed five hundred pounds, and would be impossible to fence. She'd have to sell the jewels out of it and leave the stripped mechanism as a prank on a cop car or something.

Frank, no longer the man of the hour, snuck off the stage and was able to get to the back of the room where Anita and Harriet were waiting.

Anita let go of Harriet and hurdled herself into his arms. "You were amazing!" she cried.

"Nice flamingo. A very close likeness," Harriet said slyly.

Frank put his arm protectively around Anita. "You never did say why you were here," he pointed out. "I'm pretty sure you weren't on the guest list."

"I'm hurt!" Harriet said. "I only wanted to see the real reveal, chat with Anita again, try her new cupcakes, rub elbows with the city's elite…"

Anita elbowed Frank. "Be nice," she chided. "We should

have just invited you," she said to Harriet magnanimously. "There's room for two of us in this town."

Harriet laughed, then she gestured at the heated bidding that was going on. "Did they just really bid two point three million dollars for that thing?"

Anita and Frank turned back to the stage as Anita squealed in glee and Harriet did what she should have done long before: fled.

CHAPTER 7

"This is a banner moment for Wilson Kinetic!" Frank exclaimed when the bidding was finally finished and the band had struck up again. The gala guests were milling around, admiring the flamingo sculpture that had gone for a cool four million dollars pledged to charity and taking turns winding the prototype of the personal variety.

For a moment, Tobias thought that Frank was going to hug him, he was so giddy and Anita was such a terrible influence on him, but he kissed Anita instead and spun her, giggling, right off of her feet.

"All those happy flamingos!" Anita agreed. "And everyone wants one for their lawns! Four million dollars!"

"It's late in the season for the reveal of the line," Tobias said quellingly. "We probably won't see a return on the factory upgrades until the next calendar year." He'd been watching for Harriet since he finished the auction, but her bright hair and glittering dress were nowhere to be seen.

"Bruno's birdbath line is doing well enough," Frank said

carelessly. "We should still be able to give decent holiday bonuses to everyone."

Frank, bless his big heart, was much more concerned with giving *away* his money than with earning it. Tobias could usually keep him reined in, but he had other things on his mind now than keeping his friend from the poorhouse. "How well do you know Harriet Slade, Anita?" he asked innocently.

"Not well at all," Anita admitted, looking around as if she'd just realized that the woman was gone. "But I just love her, don't you? She's so stylish and funny."

Considering how little she'd said to him, Tobias wasn't sure that he would have labeled her as funny, but stylish definitely worked. "Where does she work?" he asked. "Which bakery, I mean?" There were three or four Patty Cakes outlets throughout the city, and a licensed coffee cart in the West River Mall.

His tone was not nearly as innocent as he'd hoped it would be.

"Why do you ask?" Frank wanted to know. His eyes twinkled. "Could you be angling for a date with my fiancée's arch-nemesis?"

Anita squealed like a tea kettle. "That would be amazing! Yes, you should date her! We can *double* date! Oh, it would be like a novel I read, where there was a big industry millionaire and his brother and these baker sisters. *We could be the baker sisters!* I've always wanted a sister! But like a *good* sister, not an evil one. It could be a double *wedding!*"

Even Frank seemed a little taken aback by Anita's enthusiasm for the idea. "I'm not sure you should be planning a wedding for Tobias," he cautioned. "He doesn't even date exclusively."

"Oh, but he will," Anita declared, as if Tobias wasn't standing right there. "He just has to meet the right girl and oh, Harriet Slade is just *perfect!* They're both so *crabby!* And, Frank, four million dollars! To think that fabulous flamingo might have been mine and I just let it slip through my fingers! I think I'm going to faint, I'd better go see what's left at the buffet before I waste away completely. The champagne has gone straight to my head."

"Sorry," Frank shot back at Tobias as Anita dragged him away. "Gotta go feed her!"

Tobias waved at his back and dodged a disgruntled senator who had dropped out of the bidding at around two million dollars to head back towards the kitchen and see if they'd run low on any refreshments or if they needed to open another crate of wine to polish off the festivities.

He was met in the back hall by two concerned-looking security guards. "Mr. Underhill," the taller of the two greeted him. "We have a problem."

Tobias was immediately all business. "What is it? Has someone damaged the flamingo?"

The guard shook his head. "No, sir. But one of the guests has been robbed."

CHAPTER 8

*H*arriet flew silently through the clear cold sky. It was that enchanted time between day and evening where the sky was dark and the horizon was still bright, casting golden light over the snow.

Between her owl, shrieking protests of love in her metaphorical ear, and Harriet's nagging memories of Tobias, of the confident tip of his head, the smirk behind the absurd beard, the earthy smell of him…Harriet was not interested in appreciating the view.

He was her *mate.*

Harriet had always figured that her chances of meeting a mate—if they even existed—were slim to nothing. She knew more shifters who hadn't than had, and the ones who had, she honestly suspected of being immature optimists who were probably confusing desire with destiny.

And Harriet didn't need to pin her happiness on some man. She would be beholden to no one, and this aching need inside of her was just a primitive hunger, some kind of evolutionary throwback that she didn't *have* to answer. She was a big girl with control over her own baser instincts.

She would just avoid anything to do with Wilson Kinetic and its charismatic CEO and this craving would pass like a midnight hankering for tacos.

WE CAN ORDER TACOS! her owl protested.

It's not a perfect analogy, Harriet tried to explain to her owl. *I'm saying that we don't HAVE to order tacos, even if we think we want them, and eventually we won't want them as much.*

WE DO WANT TACOS! her owl insisted. *TOBIAS TACOS!*

Harriet could not really deny that she would very much *like* a Tobias taco. She made the mistake of imagining his arms around her, his meat between her shells, his hot sauce… and she nearly crashed into the side of her condo building because she forgot to flap her wings.

She scrambled to a stop on her balcony and shifted back into her human form, her heels sliding in the slushy snow as she yanked the glass door open to stomp into her condo.

OUR TACOS ARE BACK THERE! her owl creeled.

Harriet closed the sliding door behind her and rested her forehead on the glass. *We can't go back to him,* she said regretfully.

Her owl made a boiling tea kettle noise of protest and fluffed herself up to twice her usual size, not the slightest bit convinced while Harriet wrenched her shoes off and went to change.

At least this trip hadn't been a complete loss. No flamingo bites or strained wings, and…

Harriet stretched her arm out in front of her. The bracelet she was wearing was a string of diamonds framing one big one, like an oversized ring. The centerpiece was probably ten carats of cushion-cut diamond, circled by smaller ones, more than thirty carats in total. The settings were white gold, and the set of two bracelets was worth about seven hundred thousand dollars at auction. Harriet had only been able to get a single bracelet from the pair, but it was still more than enough to pay for the frustrations of the evenings.

And frustrations they were. Harriet felt so tightly wound that she threatened to snap like a harp string. A mate was just a terrible inconvenience. She didn't believe in true love, and she didn't need a *boyfriend* like a weight around her neck. Tobias did dangerous things to her heart, but she knew that finding a mate couldn't just fix all the things that made her an awful idea.

He might be a great guy, and perfect for her, but that didn't make her perfect for him.

She was damaged and dangerous, and the very best thing that she could do for Tobias was stay away from him altogether.

CHAPTER 9

Tobias frowned over the security footage.

"Can't you make the picture bigger?" he asked. "Add pixels or whatever they do in CSI?"

The security guard winced. "It doesn't work that way, sir."

Councilwoman Henderson was adamant that she had both bracelets during the entire auction. "My husband joked about pawning them for the flamingo," she told Tobias and the police. "I am quite certain I had them both then. And when I got my coat, one of them was gone."

The event hall had already been scoured. "I didn't drop it," the councilwoman complained. "It has a foolproof clasp. You don't wear a bracelet of *this* value with a simple hook connection. Someone *stole* it."

Frank was making the rounds of remaining guests, asking whether anyone had seen anything, trying to figure out who had been near Mrs. Henderson during the window of opportunity and keep gossip at a minimum. Tobias wryly thought that Frank was not the best choice for keeping a crowd calm, and they probably ought to switch places, but Mrs.

Henderson was insisting on Tobias, and Tobias was necessary to keep *her* calm.

"We'll find the bracelet," he promised her, not conceding that it had actually been stolen. "Ah, here you are, coming into the frame now."

She was sailing through the crowd like a clipper ship, people parting before her, her husband in her wake, but Tobias was actually watching another figure on the screen.

Harriet was there, clustered with the other people waiting at the coat check. Tobias reminded himself that he was supposed to be finding a jewel thief, not mooning over an infuriating woman. He shouldn't even be able to recognize her, in that sea of people, but the line of her neck and the pile of her hair was unmistakable, even in black and white, fuzzy and indistinct. It was something in the way she carried herself, something about her presence, not just the shiny dress that she was wearing.

Tobias reminded himself that he was watching Mrs. Henderson, even as the two crossed paths briefly. There was Mrs. Henderson at the coat check, getting her furs, as Harriet swirled into her own coat at the front door.

"Wait, go back." Tobias didn't explain himself, just let the security guard rewind the image and play it forward more slowly.

"There, see? It's gone!" Mrs. Henderson said in triumph, pointing to her bare arm as she accepted the fur coat over the counter.

But Tobias was looking at the other corner of the screen, at the indistinct form of Harriet as she pulled her own coat on, a bracelet clear on her arm a brief moment before it was covered by her sleeve. The video was not of high enough quality that it was at all possible to discern *what* bracelet she was wearing, but Tobias vividly remembered that her arms had been unadorned that evening. "Go back again," he said, just as the video got to Mrs. Henderson breaking into hysterics.

There was nothing in the video to point to Harriet. No one else in the room even noticed her on the tape as a suspect, though they speculated about several other people that stopped to talk with Mrs. Henderson or even exchange chummy hugs. "It couldn't be Victoria Hennings!" Mrs. Henderson said with a gasp. "It *couldn't* be."

Harriet herself barely brushed against the councilwoman in the crowd once, not changing trajectories in the slightest, not pausing to chat. To all appearances, she made a beeline for the coat check and then left the party, not even looking at the victim.

Tobias agonized over saying something. It was not enough to make any kind of case that Harriet was wearing an indistinct bracelet. Nothing in the footage was damning enough to point a finger, every other woman in the picture was wearing a bracelet, nearly all of them had *more* opportunity. Neither the police officer or security guard took a second look at Harriet.

"Go back again," he said, hoping for a clear shot of Harriet's wrist before their paths crossed. He couldn't even get that much clarification—there were always other people in the way, there was too much going on—and there was no hint that Harriet had made the snatch. There was a moment she *might* have, but it was so brief and smooth that Tobias found himself doubting she could have pulled it off.

Mrs. Henderson draped herself dramatically in the chair. "This is a *tragedy*," she said in tones of despair. "I paid seven hundred *thousand* dollars for those bracelets."

"You still have one," her mousy husband tried to comfort her.

"It was a pair," Mrs. Henderson said crossly. "It isn't worth nearly as much alone."

"We'll get a description out to the pawn shops and jewelers," the police officer promised. "They won't be able to fence it easily."

"They could pry the diamonds out," Tobias suggested.

Mrs. Henderson gave a moan of dismay.

The police officer gave Tobias a sour look. "They could, but not many people buy unset diamonds. Councilwoman Henderson, I assure you, we will find the culprit and return your jewelry before it can be dismantled. We've got the limos that were leaving all stopped at the gates and we'll search every one of them."

But Harriet was already gone, probably by wing and not by car, Tobias thought, and she wasn't on the guest list to follow up with.

It was the perfect crime.

CHAPTER 10

"How was the dress?" Eva asked when Harriet walked into the office above the Patty Cakes bakery on Tuesday morning.

"It worked," Harriet said sharply. The room smelled like cinnamon and sugar, and Harriet could not stop thinking about the spicy cupcake that Tobias had offered her.

Eva wilted at Harriet's tone and Harriet felt bad for her distraction and short-temper. "I had six people ask me who my designer was," she added kindly. "And I got several phone numbers." But not Tobias's. Not that she wanted it.

Eva beamed. Harriet was torn between wishing that she could protect the young woman from every slight and hard knock and wanting to toughen her up so that she wasn't hurt so easily. No one got far in this world by being sensitive.

Eva was madly talented as a seamstress, and Harriet had recognized her potential the moment she shyly came in for an interview at the bakery wearing a handmade dress. After talking to Eva for an hour and realizing that she was sleeping in her car, Harriet offered her a job on the spot—not as a baker, but as a personal assistant…with a few extra duties and some under-the-table perks. Harriet needed fancy clothing and an extra hand with her hair once in a while, and Eva needed a place to stay and access to a sewing machine. Harriet remodeled one of the back rooms of the suite into a well-lit sewing studio with top of the line machines and a comfortable fold-out couch, even though it wasn't technically zoned for residential use, leaving the lobby ostensibly for Patty Cakes Bakeries.

Harriet knew that it was only a matter of time before Eva outstripped her position as Harriet's tailor. Her designs were inspired, and Harriet was already cultivating the contacts that she would need to help Eva rise through the ranks of celebrity designers, teasing the right people with the confections that she wore, leaving just enough mystery behind her to intrigue and captivate. They would be a perfect team, with her social savvy and Eva's design brilliance.

"Was it…a profitable night?"

Harriet often wondered if she'd made the right move taking Eva into her confidence. Eva blushed too easily and was achingly naive. But Harriet couldn't explain her need for memorable high society clothing, even as the owner of a small chain of successful bakeries. When Eva had observed that there wasn't much traffic to her bakery, considering the profits they posted, Harriet had come clean about the fact that Patty Cakes was a method for her to launder money for her actual career of grand thievery. Something about Eva's forthright innocence had prompted a full confession.

Anita reminded her of Eva, Harriet realized, with her sunny joyfulness. Eva, fortunately, was much quieter and shyer, and not given to so many clingy hugs.

"Profitable enough," Harriet said off-handedly. She had the bracelet she'd stolen in her purse, and planned to meet with one of her jewelers later that day once she'd seen how much press there was about the theft. It wasn't going to go unnoticed, but was it going to be a quiet file with the police or a big public outcry? It had been risky to steal the bracelet after her identity had been discovered, but there should still be nothing to point the crime to her. She wondered with a stab of guilt whether Frank and Tobias would have to take the brunt of the bad press as hosts of the gala, then reminded herself fiercely that she owed them *nothing*.

In the meantime, there was still plenty of year-end accounting paperwork to get through for the bakery, which the IRS didn't understand was a front (and Harriet hoped to keep it that way), and she had two more holiday parties to hit before Christmas, so her weekends were booked.

Harriet retreated into her office with a cup of coffee and thought about taking a cold shower, because her owl was still nagging her about Tobias, *Tobias*, TOBIAS and even her usual solitary methods of taking the edge off of her appetites that morning had not made a dent in her hunger.

This will pass, she told herself and her owl fiercely. *We're not going to see him again, so it doesn't matter.*

Her owl clacked her beak in displeasure.

The phone on her desk gave a buzz as she was still trying to decide how much to massage her numbers for July. "Ms. Slade?" Eva was only so formal when someone had come up to the office itself, which almost never happened; Harriet hired terrifying managers that could handle even the most disgruntled clients and was clear that she didn't want to be bothered unnecessarily.

"Yes, Eva?"

"There's a Tobias Underhill to see you. He says he has… unfinished business with you."

Harriet's owl shrieked in joy.

CHAPTER 11

Tobias was very good with data. He quickly figured out where Harriet lived and what she drove and easily deduced her base of operation—the West Fifth branch had a suite of offices on the floor above the bakery. He didn't want to show up at her condo doorstep; that seemed more than a little presumptuous, but he also didn't want to wait until she'd had a chance to forget their meeting. So he arrived late in the morning on Tuesday, making the timing just right to casually ask her out to lunch if they got to that point.

He thought about what he'd found out about Harriet as he pulled into the little parking lot. Her car—a very nice sedan—was there, plus one beat-up Subaru. Harriet didn't have a social media presence, besides pages for Patty Cakes that were irregularly updated. The hours of this branch of the bakery were limited—she wasn't open on Mondays at all, though she employed enough staff for a comparable business to be open full time every day.

Her business record was clean, with no violations or warnings of any type on her license. The reviews online were the standard mix of "My favorite bakery!" and "Terrible biscuits," plus just a few bizarre reviews that sounded like the customer was reviewing a dental service while they were still hopped up on laughing gas.

Going back further, Tobias had been unable to find any public school records for Harriet Slade, either college or secondary graduations. Had she enrolled in a private school? Formal education wasn't a strict requirement for a successful entrepreneur; it was possible that she had simply bypassed that formality. He had a request with a detective friend for more background, quietly under the table so he didn't spook her.

Public records for Patty Cakes suggested that it performed brilliantly; Harriet had been able to open four branches within a few years of opening her doors and the taxes she paid the city indicated booming business.

The parking lot didn't particularly suggest that booming business, nor did the empty bakery.

An old woman in an apron with short, white-streaked hair was filling up a candy jar and she glared at Tobias with obvious dislike before scuttling back into the kitchen, sideways like a crab. The man at the counter had a magenta mohawk and a dozen piercings, plus a spiked collar. He did, however, know his fritters from his empanadas, and Tobias graciously bought two of each.

"I'd like to speak to Harriet Slade," he said, as he tucked a twenty dollar bill into the tip jar.

The man behind the counter raised an eyebrow and sent out the manager, instead.

Harriet's manager was an amazon of a woman with fore-arms like full-sized hams and Tobias suspected that she was used to intimidating customers out of their complaints. All of Harriet's hires seemed to be on the sketchy side, and Tobias would eat his hat if this one hadn't at one point worked for the mob. Was Harriet running an entire ring of thieves from the tax shelter of her bakery chain? Was Harriet herself a *part* of the mob? Was it possible that the bracelet theft was part of something larger and more personal? Councilwoman Henderson probably had plenty of political enemies; her crackdown on crime had cast a wide and unpopular net.

The plot was definitely thickening.

"I'd like to speak with Harriet Slade," Tobias repeated. He didn't think a bribe would get very far with this woman.

"Ms. Slade is *particular* about her visitors," the ham-armed woman said, giving Tobias an appraising rake from head to toe.

Tobias grinned up at her. "She *should* be," he said approvingly. "But I'm quite sure she's eager to see me again. We have some unfinished business regarding the Wilson Kinetic Charity Gala." He decide a wink was too much, but a waggle of eyebrows gave a suggestion of the kind of business he might be meaning.

Would that be enough to get him past this behemoth? Should he lay in a pointed hint about diamonds or bracelets? Tobias preferred to hold valuable information close to his chest while he could and the last thing he wanted to do was scare Harriet into running.

Ham-arms frowned at him, looking unswayed, and Tobias gave her a slow, sly smile. "I promise to tell her you were terrifying and nearly frightened me into leaving."

That earned him a surprised chuckle and she pointed Tobias to a stairwell with a chain across the door. "At the top on the left," she said briefly.

The stairs were carpeted and silent under Tobias's feet. He ducked under the chain and strode up.

He caught the receptionist by surprise, and she put down the swath of cloth she was embroidering and stared at Tobias in alarm. "What do you want?" she blurted, clutching the desk. "I mean, ah, can I help you?" She looked like she was ready to bolt away.

"I'm here to see Ms. Slade," Tobias said carefully. "Tobias Underhill. We have some unfinished business and she's probably expecting me."

Honestly, it surprised him that Harriet *had* a receptionist. This woman was very shy and scattered and it took her several moments to figure out how to use the phone on her desk to buzz Harriet. "Ms. Slade?"

Harriet sounded very patient over the intercom. "Yes, Eva?"

Eva stared at Tobias with great, round blue eyes. "There's a Tobias Underhill to see you. He says he has…unfinished business with you."

There was a muffled squeak and no answer for so long that Eva looked in consternation at her phone and started pushing buttons at random. "Sorry, I think I must have, ah, hung up on her? I should, um, you shouldn't…"

Tobias was already going for the door that Eva was casting desperate looks toward. "Thank you, Eva!" he said expansively. "Don't let me interrupt your beautiful work."

She looked down at her embroidery in absolute alarm as Tobias reached for the door handle and blew her a flirty kiss.

Tobias had told himself for several days that he was only investigating Harriet because she was his primary suspect in a high profile theft that had occurred under his watch, that his interest in her was purely professional. It wasn't that he was enamored of her, or flattered by the way she had seemed desperate for him and just as desperate to deny her own attraction.

But his reaction at the sight of her—that tilt of her head, the defensive set of her jaw!—suggested at once that he was the desperate one.

She was so beautiful and so alive, her eyes flashing as she started to rise to her feet, and Tobias had never wanted anything so much in his life. His breath came fast and his blood flowed hot. He wouldn't have cared if she'd stolen the jeweled flamingo itself.

He put his bakery bag down and settled himself deliberately in the chair across from her with a slow smile, pretending that she hadn't just set his body on fire and hoping that his erection wasn't obvious. "Ms. Slade, how lovely to see you again. I hope you are enjoying this fine weather?"

"The weather?" Harriet froze halfway to standing and sank back into her chair with a puzzled glance out the window. It was somewhere between snow and sleet outside.

"The weather," Tobias repeated. "A series of meteorological events caused by wind patterns and changing temperatures, largely driven by seasonal cycles caused by the tilt of our world on its rotational axis."

"Rotational axis?" She closed her eyes and drew in a deep breath. "How can I help you, Mr. Underhill?"

"So formal," Tobias teased her. He realized that some of the reason that she looked so different was that she was wearing glasses. They didn't seem to be a high prescription, and Tobias wondered if they weren't a simple affectation. Did she think that it worked like it did with Superman, and she was Clark Kent wearing them, completely anonymous? Her hair was also less bright and more natural. The combination, along with her pedestrian clothing, made her look like a different woman, but Tobias didn't think she looked any less lovely. "Won't you call me Tobias?"

"Tobias?" She said it like it was a question.

"That's the name my mother gave me. Do you mind if I call you Harriet?"

"Harriet?" she said faintly.

"I understand that's your name."

She looked furious for a moment, though Tobias thought that was more aimed at herself than at him. "Yes, that's my name. What do you *want*?"

Although it hadn't been his first purpose, it seemed very natural to admit, "I'd like to take you on a date."

CHAPTER 12

"*A* date?" Harriet knew that she was going to have to stop answering his questions with foolish echoes at some point, but this was apparently not that moment. Her owl was cooing in her head like a lovesick dove, making it very hard to think.

"I don't date," she said flatly.

That wasn't entirely true. She dated plenty, but it was always with purpose—men with the keycards she needed for breaking into museums and art galleries, or someone who could get her a ticket to a fancy gala or use her as their plus one. She never actually slept with them because that was against her strict code of honor, but it was pretty amazing what a woman wearing a slinky gown could accomplish with a shy, promising smile and a tongue across her lips.

Tobias licked his own lips thoughtfully, like he'd heard her thoughts, and Harriet cursed what that did to *her*. She'd guessed right that he was clean-shaved underneath the awful white Santa beard that he'd been wearing, and his jaw was a thing of poetry, begging to be touched.

She needed to get rid of this guy sooner than later,

because he was badly under her skin, and that was entirely too close to her heart.

"Maybe we could—"

Harriet cut him off before he could suggest coffee or lunch or something harmless and twee like a walk in the park on a sleeting December day. "Look, I'm not sure what kind of moment you thought we had—"

(Her owl was happy to supply a distracting idea of the kind of moment they *could* have.)

"—but I have a bakery to run and no time for a relationship, so if you aren't here to buy cupcakes, you can kindly get out of my office."

Tobias's eyes flashed at her and his mouth curved up in a grin. "Very well, I'm here to buy cupcakes."

Dammit, she'd given him an out.

Or an *in*, as the case may be.

In, her owl agreed happily. *In **and** out.*

"Let me get you an order form," Harriet said between gritted teeth, not willing to let her owl drag her down that train of thought. She yanked a desk drawer open and found the folder of sickening pink order forms fringed in hearts. "Here."

Tobias took the form, and then used it as an invitation to lean forward on her desk, looking thoughtfully over the options. "Do you have a pen?" he asked maddeningly.

Harriet found that the pen cup on her desk had a hair stick, a spoon, and seven paperclips, but no pens. Her drawer was no better.

"There's one in my purse," she remembered, reaching for it. She realized, just before she opened it, that the diamond bracelet she'd filched on her way out of the flamingo shifter's gala was still in there, and she was careful to keep it open away from Tobias's view. He was pretending to study his order form, but Harriet recognized that he was mostly watching her. She knew that not-a-look because she had mastered it.

"Here." She thrust the pen at him and was both glad and disappointed that he managed to take it from her without touching her hand.

"I'll be needing several thousand cupcakes for our next charity fundraiser," Tobias said, eyeing his overpriced choices.

"Doesn't Frank Wilson already have a pet baker?" Harriet told herself she wasn't jealous of Anita. Anita was a twit and Harriet didn't need or want a relationship like that.

"We're an equal opportunity business," Tobias said officiously. "I'm collecting competitive bids for the event."

"There's a 20% administrative fee for jobs of two thousand cupcakes and up," Harriet said impulsively, hoping that would price her out of 'competitive.' "I'd have to pay my staff overtime." The last thing she wanted with this guy was his *business.*

(Her owl knew exactly what kind of business she wanted.)

"We'll do three thousand," Tobias said. "Any extras can be given to the food bank."

"You don't have to…"

"That will be perfect," Tobias stopped her. "I'll arrange for samples and have someone contact you if you make the cut."

If she made the *cut?*

Harriet was outraged. He was the one who'd come in here, talking about the weather and asking her on a date and now he was acting like she was the one being judged. It didn't matter that her cupcakes were actually pretty pedestrian, or that she didn't give a pellet for his opinion of her bakery and didn't actually want his contract. "Listen up, you pretentious tool, I don't need your business and I don't want your charity. If you want to support the unfortunate I suggest you find a non-profit for *lost puppies*. Maybe *they'll* lick your bell-bangled boots."

Harriet knew that she'd gone too far the moment the words left her mouth and she cursed her short temper and quick tongue. Her owl fluffed up and tried to bury its head under a wing.

Tobias stared at her for a long moment and then burst out in a shout of laughter. "Harriet Slade, you are a national treasure. We'll do four thousand cupcakes if your samples stand up to your tongue and be glad of the opportunity." He stood, gathering his paper bakery bag, and took the order form. "I've taken enough of your time this morning. I look forward to doing business with you."

Harriet got to her feet as well, not entirely sure what was happening. When he thrust a hand at her, apparently to shake, her body betrayed her with a flush of desire. She didn't dare touch him, so she glared at him instead. "Margo will see you out," she snarled.

Tobias managed to make her refusal to shake his hand the subject of a knowing smirk, damn him, and he bowed, instead. "I'll be in touch!" he said merrily.

Then he was gone, and Harriet could sink, weak-kneed, back into her chair.

Touch! her owl hooted happily. *He'll be in touch! He'll touch us!*

"Your Harriet woman is a real piece of work," Antonio told Tobias as he settled in the seat across Tobias's desk.

Tobias bristled in defense. "Take that back," he snarled.

Antonio put his hands up in surprise. "No offense. You were the one who wanted the dirt on her. And it was not easy to find, let me tell you. Her records were sealed when she hit her majority, and she changed her name. I had to pull serious strings to get the deets."

Tobias's curiosity overcame his protectiveness and he cursed himself for betraying his irrational emotions to Antonio. "Just tell me," he said flatly. It was probably too late to redeem his image of being aloof. He should have kept this to a phone call, but he worried that whatever Antonio dug up would be incriminating enough that Tobias didn't want a possible recording of it.

"She was an orphan, left at the fire station when she was just a few months old. Went through the foster system but got bounced out of every family she was placed with. Sometimes in just days. Spent time in juvie, some in rehab. Petty theft, vandalism, harassment, possession, this girl did it all. The weird part is that when she hit eighteen and her records were sealed, she went squeaky clean. I mean spotless. If she committed any crimes or did anything harder than cigarettes, she didn't let anyone catch her at it. As far as the public is concerned, this woman is a by-the-book modestly successful entrepreneur with a totally clear conscience. She donates to charities, animal rescue and such. Every bit of it is too good to be true. So, I did a little more digging."

Tobias was still stuck on the part where Harriet had been abandoned as a baby. That certainly explained some of her prickly defensiveness. He thought about his own life, his big extended family, his busybody mother. He'd lost his father when he were young, but how much worse would it have been to have no family whatsoever?

Antonio was still waiting for a prompt to go on. "So, did you want to know what else I found?"

"Yes," Tobias said shortly. He wanted to know everything about Harriet that there was to know.

"I thought she might be in the hole, that maybe she was underwater on Patty Cakes. But what's weird is that she has no debt. Not a shred of it. There's no sign of where an orphaned girl fresh out of juvie would have gotten the startup for a bakery, let alone the training to run it so successfully that she can buy her properties outright in a matter of years. She owns her car, her condo, the entire building that each branch of her bakery is in. She's somehow making a lot of money, and while her bakery can explain some of it, her numbers are a little…too good to be true."

"Some kind of underground trade?" Tobias posited. He didn't want to believe that Harriet was dealing in drugs, but he had a strong case for stolen goods. He hated that *wealthy patron* was still a possibility. Or maybe she had off-the-books debt? He hadn't eliminated the mob, yet.

"Those fancy dresses you were curious about?" Antonio had a portfolio full of photographs. Harriet in a slinky red thing. Harriet in a crystal-encrusted ball gown. Harriet in a simple white gown that made Tobias think the dirtiest thoughts.

"All I can say is that she doesn't buy them from a dealer. As far as I can tell, she's getting them privately, and she's making people mad with curiosity about her designer, teasing that she can put them in touch, but not actually coming forward with a name."

"You think she's running some kind of dress design for her side money?"

"Not for a moment," Antonio said. "As far as I can tell, she's not selling any of them. I think she's got some other kind of racket going, but balls if I can tell what it is."

Jewel theft. Art heists. She was using the bakeries to launder her more devious earnings. Steal something valuable, fence it quietly, declare the earnings as untraceable cash sales through a chain of totally innocuous bakeries, and she could live the lifestyle she was stealing with a completely clean tax record. It held up perfectly to a surface scrutiny. Maybe it was a whole ring of thieves, Tobias guessed, remembering the sketchy staff at her primary branch.

"Antonio," Tobias said seriously. "I want you to forget everything you found."

"You want the glory of fingering this dame yourself?" Antonio guessed.

Tobias abruptly thought of a completely different kind of glorious fingering and had to force his traitorous brain back onto his train of thought.

"I'm happy to pay generously for the information you've

found," Tobias said mildly. "I just need you to guarantee that it goes no further, for any reason."

Antonio gave him a skeptical look. "Yeah, okay, mate. Discretion is my middle name."

CHAPTER 14

"Good night, Eva!" Harriet called up the stairs.

But Eva had her music up loud and was buried in her work already, a brilliant ball gown with a butterfly wing motif that, even half-finished, looked like it had been stolen straight out of a fairyland. That would be the dress that opened doors for her, Harriet knew. She was going to have to finalize her plans for Eva's big reveal and lose her as an assistant very soon. Not that Eva had ever been a particularly outstanding assistant—Harriet was fortunately quite accomplished at managing her own affairs and Eva's technical position was really only a formality to excuse her employment. She'd need her own quarters (legally zoned for residency), and her own life soon enough in order to go public.

Harriet told herself that she was only going to miss Eva as a resource, not as a friend. Harriet didn't have friends, she had business opportunities. It wasn't like she hadn't gained plenty for herself by encouraging Eva in her art and getting her the supplies and training she needed. It was only a logical transaction, and she didn't need or want Eva's worshipful affection. Feelings were nothing but trouble, and the faster she kicked the girl from the nest, the better it would be for all of them.

It was still early afternoon—Harriet used her early opening as an excuse to close just after noon, and she was looking forward to crossing her last holiday event off that weekend so she could get back to ignoring Christmas. Her fence thought he could get her a hundred grand for the single bracelet, and that, on top of what she could skim from the Panzer's Christmas ball would be enough to get a solid, legitimate place for Eva to start her shop. She was running her mind over the marks she might expect to meet there with so much of her attention that she was startled when her owl suddenly shrieked in her ear as she was locking the door.

Mate!

"Why Harriet Slade, fancy meeting you here." Tobias managed to look perfectly innocent, but Harriet wasn't the slightest bit fooled. She was, however, extremely bothered by her own excitement at the sight of him. She should not be fluttering like a chick because of some stupid long-haired hippy. Even a brilliant, billionaire hippy. She should not be so distracted that she hadn't noticed his approach.

"It's the parking lot of my bakery at closing time," Harriet pointed out. "It's not that much of a shock that I'm here. Are you stalking me?" It was awkward standing a step above him, exaggerating the difference in their height, but Harriet was not willing to step down to meet him.

"You wound me," Tobias said, stepping up onto the shop stoop himself despite the small space. He peered in through the glass door. "Are you closed already? I had hoped to pick up a cupcake sample to bring to Frank. Your bid is in the running for our next event, and naturally I don't plan to settle for second best."

"Our hours are posted," Harriet said shortly. He was

standing entirely too close on the small stoop and doing very distracting things to her calm. Weirdest of all, he had a full beard today, which ought to have been impossible to grow since his clean-shaven visit to her office just a few days before. It wasn't long, but it was certainly full. Was it fake? Harriet resisted her urge to reach out and tug on it. "You'll have to come back when we're open."

"Or I could use my manly wiles to get you to let me in for a sample after hours," Tobias suggested.

"You put a lot of stock in those manly wiles, don't you," Harriet said, laughing despite herself.

"They've served me well," Tobias said without a shred of humility. "Harriet, I have a bold request for you."

Was he going to ask to kiss her? Harriet hated the jolt of hope and anticipation that the wild idea gave her. He hadn't been shy about the fact that he was interested in her, but he'd been a gentleman so far, so it was an absurd idea and she chided herself for even thinking of it.

And worse, for *wanting* it.

"Would you tell me your dress designer?"

Was that all? Harriet had a moment of jealousy. He was asking about *Eva?*

"She's a well-kept secret," Harriet said evasively.

"Like you yourself," Tobias suggested.

Harriet forced herself to relax. He didn't know her secrets. He was just prying for a crack in her defenses. And he wasn't going to find that. She knew how to handle nosy people and how to deflect curiosity. She'd gotten rid of persistent suitors before. All she had to do was get her feet back under herself.

She forced a sparkling laugh. "I'm no secret," she said humbly. "Just a baker who's been lucky in business."

"You don't use your real name at the gala events you attend."

"A silly conceit," Harriet said carelessly. How many events did he know about? Was it enough to put together a profile of her activity? It wasn't that she thought she'd gone completely unrecognized, but she did try to keep her personas neatly separated. Mousy, unimpressive Harriet Slade was just a quiet businesswoman. She wasn't on guest lists and wouldn't presume to flirt with senators.

"It must have been annoying to have Anita recognize you, when you crashed the party that didn't happen."

Harriet stared at him in challenge, not allowing her gaze to waver. There was nothing incriminating in what he'd discovered. Other obsessive types had pursued her to her real name, but there was nothing else to find. To all appearances, she was just indulging in a one-off fairy tale evening out. She came into their lives and left just as quickly. People only remembered her hair, and whatever she was wearing. If they pursued her past the midnight hour, all that they found was a disappointingly ordinary businesswoman who paled into unimportance.

But here was Tobias again, after he'd seen her in her everyday clothes, with her reading glasses and her faded ginger hair. Why *was* he here? And how did she get rid of him, before she did something she'd regret forever?

She let her eyes slide away from him and she laughed softly and shook her head. "Fine, you found me out," she said with a shrug. "I wanted an evening of glamour and I wasn't invited, so I dressed up and pretended to be someone important for a few hours. It's over now and I assure you, I won't give Wilson Kinetics any further trouble." Her posture was artfully meek and she thought it wasn't too much to scuff a toe of her boot sheepishly in the slush. "I'm honestly not looking for Prince Charming and I'm not nearly as interesting as you think I am."

If he had been anyone else, that would have been the end

of it entirely. Her shy confession would have dispelled whatever mystery she held for him, her gentle rebuff would have worked, and he wouldn't want anything more.

The first problem was that Harriet actually wanted this one.

The second problem was that Tobias didn't look like he was the slightest bit convinced of her innocence. He was still regarding her thoughtfully, like he was trying to decide his next move.

And worst of all, Harriet wished she truly *was* innocent for him. She wanted to be uncomplicated and available, so that she could simply *let* herself fall in love and be swept away. She'd never wanted a mate until she saw what Anita and Frank had, and however absurd and disgusting they were, nothing had ever struck so deep into her soul like watching them fall in love.

But Harriet was nothing like Anita. She was prickles and pain, bad judgment and layers of armor. As sure as her owl was that they were meant to be, Harriet knew that it was only that Tobias was everything that she wanted, not that she could be good for him. She wasn't good for anyone and never would be.

Her role in the fairy tale was fairy godmother at best.

Or maybe the pumpkin.

"That's regrettable," Tobias said.

Harriet had to track back to what she'd said before. "That I'm not that interesting?"

"That you're not looking for Prince Charming," Tobias said with a smirk. "I mean, here I am. It would be very convenient if you were."

Harriet made an inelegant snort as she tried not to laugh. "You have an unbelievable ego, don't you!"

"It's one of my better qualities," Tobias agreed.

"Your *ego* is a *better quality*?" Harriet sniffed but could not entirely hide her amusement. "I'm not sure what that says about your other attributes."

"Possibly that they are all above average," Tobias suggested. "I invite you to find out and rank them yourself."

His tone was not subtle, hinting at exactly which attributes Harriet might enjoy investigating and Harriet caught herself blushing and hating herself for that visible weakness. Her owl was cooing and she was a dangerous mix of keyed up and disarmed by Tobias's humor.

"Oh, hold on," Tobias said, and he reached a hand for Harriet. When she froze instead of deflecting him or fleeing like she really ought to do, he plucked a non-pareil from her hair.

"You had a sprinkle in your hair," he said, holding it out to her.

He was so close, and she was so on fire that she had to bend down and kiss him.

CHAPTER 15

Tobias was expecting to win a kiss from Harriet after a long and fraught courtship, not the simple act of removing candy from a lock of her hair. He was so caught by surprise that for a moment he couldn't do anything but let her lips fall on his hungrily.

Then he realized in a flash what exactly was happening and he opened his mouth to kiss her back and take her face in his hands, forgetting that he was still holding the sprinkle.

When she jerked back, like she'd just become aware of what her body had done without her direction, the nonpareil was stuck to her cheek.

"I didn't mean to do that," she squawked.

"I think you did," Tobias said gently. He could still taste her on his lips, the spicy, salty flavor of her like a meal he'd been craving for a month. She was so much woman in one person, so much personality packed into her gorgeous curves. He couldn't imagine anyone else half as intriguing… and he had never had a kiss so hot.

He reached to peel the sprinkle from her cheek and she flinched away as if he'd drawn a knife on her. Before he could even abort the touch, she was springing away, up into the air with spread wings, surprisingly silent as she beat up into the air and away from him as a large, pale owl.

Tobias watched her with an ache of longing until she vanished into the washed out sky, lost in the city skyline.

She was so conflicted. He could tell that she wanted him, even before she'd kissed him like a burst of fireworks, and yet she seemed absolutely determined to resist him. Why? What made him an unsuitable partner in her eyes?

A thought like a lightning bolt struck him. Could he be her mate?

Gnomes didn't have mates, but shifters did, and Harriet Slade was obviously a shifter. It might explain her irresistible attraction to him, though Tobias knew that he could have that effect on people without supernatural power. He was a fine-looking, well-built specimen, with the added allure of great wealth and sharp wit. It was possible that Harriet simply had good taste along with her keen intelligence.

Tobias was more sure than ever now that it was Harriet that had stolen the bracelet. She had the reflexes and the background. She had the underworld contacts. But he couldn't figure out her motives. She didn't strike him as the kind of person who hoarded wealth and she didn't live luxuriously. She had a nice car, but her condo was modest and her lifestyle—aside from her sideline crashing balls in designer clothing—was understated. She already owned her property outright. What was she doing with her stolen goods?

Frowning at the car that Harriet had probably not intended to leave in the parking lot, Tobias pulled his phone from his coat pocket and thoughtfully dialed Antonio.

"Tony," the call was answered.

"Antonio, I know I told you to drop the investigation on Harriet Slade, but I have a few more questions."

Antonio's silence was unexpected and Tobias was experienced enough to recognize it as uncomfortable. "What did you find out?" he demanded.

"A few things," Antonio said reluctantly. "She's been setting other people up with businesses, too. Legitimate, as far as I can dig, and you know how far I can dig. One of her cupcake bakers got settled in a little jewelry shop selling his own designs. One of her prior janitors is running an art store. Looks like she finds down-on-their-luck crafters and artists and hands them opportunities."

Lost puppies, Tobias thought. "Did she keep them in her name?" he wanted to know.

"Nope. Fully owned and operated by the individuals. She's got no fingers in those pots that I can tease out at all. Doesn't even take credit for it, she makes it look like weird, random luck."

Tobias didn't really believe in luck. He did believe in good-hearted people, and he wondered how much of Harriet's prickly exterior was cultivated to keep people from seeing that.

There was another mystery here. "So, why were you still looking for this, Antonio?" he asked, keeping his tone carefully mild.

Antonio was quiet for too long.

"Someone else is asking about her," Tobias guessed. If he had figured her out, and if Harriet had been doing this as long as he guessed she had, it wasn't unlikely that she'd caught the attention of someone else.

Antonio didn't deny it, which was answer enough for Tobias.

"Here's what you're going to do, Antonio," he said, letting a thread of ice into his tone. "You're going to tell your client that you got a better offer, and I'm going to pay you twice what they are, and twice that again to them if they forget everything they think they know. But if I see or sniff or hear about anyone else looking into Harriet Slade, they are going to get a metric ton of angry billionaire gnome in their business and that is the last thing they want. She's under my protection now, with everything that comes with that."

Tobias hung up before Antonio could answer. His fingers were cold and he stomped his feet to warm them. The heat of Harriet's kiss still warmed his lips, but the rest of him was flirting with frostbite.

CHAPTER 16

She'd kissed him.

Like a complete idiot with no concept of boundaries, Harriet had fallen for his brief proximity and the heady, sexy smell of him and lost control of her owl's instincts for one critical, catastrophic moment. Her mouth found his as if it had been drawn there like a magnet, and he was exactly as yielding and firm as he ought to be, his breath hot in her mouth when he took her face in his hands.

She knew that she was lost, completely and utterly. There was no Harriet now, only this helpless skin of her that was wholly his.

It took all of her will to fight her way back from the terrible mistake and yank herself out of his grasp.

Her owl was chirping, happy with even that much surrender, but Harriet was appalled as she flew through the afternoon winter gloom. How could she let this happen? She was only leading him down a path that she didn't dare travel. There was no happy ending for them. It was cruel to give him and her owl that kind of hope. She'd even been startled into shifting out in broad daylight.

Ours! Her owl sang. *Our mate! Bring him dead mice and dance!*

Harriet landed with a crash on her balcony. Tobias was terrible for her concentration as well as her flight skills. She needed him out from under her skin in the worst way.

Her phone rang as Harriet was undressing to take a bath and possibly drown herself in it to stop from thinking about mates and dead mice. She had to shimmy the rest of the way out of her shirt to answer it, glancing at the number with hope and feeling her heart fall when it was only Eva.

Scolding herself for hoping it was an unknown number with Tobias's voice at the other end, she answered brusquely, "Yes?"

"Oh, sorry, Ms. Slade, ma'am. I didn't want to disturb you at home."

Harriet gentled her voice. "It's fine, Eva. What is it?"

"It's just, the door wasn't locked and your car was still here, but you weren't and I wasn't sure if there was a problem or if I should lock up or if you were…okay. I didn't know what to do."

Harriet put her face in one hand. Tobias had distracted her so thoroughly she hadn't finished locking up, and of course her car was still in the parking lot since she'd shifted in a panic and flown home. "Nothing's wrong, Eva, I just came home by an alternate method and must have forgotten to lock up. It's been a busy week, I'm more tired than I thought. Thanks for checking in. Everything's fine." The lies flowed off her tongue. *Everything's fine.*

Eva gave a sigh of relief at the other end of the line. "Oh, good. Thanks, Ms. Slade. I was just worried. I've got the alterations for your gown this weekend finished, I'll just need to check the fit tomorrow."

"I'm sure it will be great," Harriet said. "I'm looking forward to seeing it. Good night." If she let her, Eva would take five years to stammer through her goodbyes, so Harriet hung up then.

She felt guilty at once for being so short. Eva was really shy and Harriet worried that she was going to have trouble going independent with her dress business. Harriet would need to find her a good manager, someone who could handle people and wouldn't let anyone run over Eva. Maybe she could part with Margo; Harriet didn't really need her own manager and Margo's talents were wasted doing the day-to-day minutiae of the bakery.

Harriet herself had a talent for theft. She had the fine motor skills for delicate work, and the acting chops—when she wasn't being distracted by handsome gnomes—to pull off any persona she set her mind to. She had a broad range of knowledge in security systems, and a way of thinking outside the box that allowed her to defeat them. She was savvy and swift-witted, able to pivot in her plans and snatch opportunity.

But her real skill was in finding lost artistic souls and setting them on the path to greatness.

She had always lamented her own lack of creative spark, but she recognized it in others. When she found herself flush with cash, building a slow, steady bank with her criminal activity and sugar-coated cover, she didn't have to look far to find her calling. Her young assistant baker at the time was a clever jeweler, designing cunning wire settings.

She set him up with a mentor through her jewel fence, found a studio with top of the line equipment, and finally got him a turnkey jewelry store that he turned into a bustling business.

Harriet appreciated that he did most of the work himself, and didn't want the kudos that he gave her, so with her next rescue, she stepped back. Her janitor, Shea got an art gallery, and Harriet did the legwork and manifested the funds, but she sheltered it all behind layers of bureaucracy—as far as Shea was concerned, she'd won a mysterious grant and Harriet simply hand-waved how the application had been submitted in the first place.

Harriet's owl instincts gave a warning jangle and she turned back to her bath just in time to stop the water before the tub overflowed. She had to open the drain for a moment in order to make enough room for herself, cursing her wool-gathering. She was making too many mistakes, being too spacey. A mate was clearly bad for her wits, and she needed Tobias out of her bloodstream in the worst way. Her lips still seemed to burn.

Her phone gave a blurble from the edge of the sink just after she had slipped into the hot water and Harriet blew frustrated bubbles before she splashed out, drying one hand before picking up the phone.

Heat sizzled through her at the text from an unknown number.

Let me take you to dinner. We still have unfinished business. The Moldave, 8 PM tomorrow.

The infuriating elf ended his message with an eggplant, leaving Harriet no doubt who it was or what he wanted.

Dammit, she had *kissed* him.

Eggplant! her owl hooted happily. *He sent an EGGPLANT. WE WANT TACOS!*

Harriet was never sure how much modern slang her owl truly understood, but she could not deny the flush of heat that washed over her, or her wave of longing. She really did want "tacos," in the worst possible way, and she feared that she was not going to have any peace until she did.

FINE, she texted back without subtlety.

CHAPTER 17

Harriet set no expectations for dinner itself.

As far as she was concerned, it was just a brief courtesy stop before she let Tobias take her up to a swanky suite a few floors above. She anticipated a short, decent meal and a little dedicated flirting, and then she'd give him the ride of his life and her owl would finally shut up about being mates and she could get back to her perfectly satisfying single life of crime.

But Tobias clearly had other plans.

"Leave your coat on," he said, when she moved to shrug out of her fur-trimmed wool overcoat as they approached the hostess stand.

Curious, Harriet aborted her unbuttoning and walked at Tobias's side all the way through the glittering restaurant. She caught sight of Councilwoman Henderson dining with a lobbyist and thought about the bracelet that she was still carrying in the lining of her purse.

She and Tobias were seated, to her surprise, on a covered private balcony just outside the actual dining room.

"You realize that it's December?" Harriet said in shock, realizing that he did indeed intend to sit outside for their dinner. She was glad that she was wearing a decent coat and that her fashionable faux fur hat was actually warm. Her shoes might prove to be a weak point, as she'd chosen heels over sensible boots, but she was a shifter, and able to tolerate temperature a little better than a normal human.

"It's not that cold tonight," Tobias said easily, holding the chair for her. "I asked them to seat us out here so that you'd have a clear escape route to the sky if you decide that a meal with me is completely untenable."

Harriet was surprised into a laugh as she sat and let Tobias tuck a napkin into her lap. "You think that I'd shift into an owl in the middle of our meal and fly away if the date was that bad?"

"Wouldn't you?" Tobias settled easily opposite from her, looking for all the world like it was perfectly normal to be wearing heavy winter wear for a formal dinner on an open balcony at near-freezing temperatures.

Harriet felt chagrined. She certainly hadn't made anything easy for Tobias. He'd been persistent and determined, but never crossed the line into being demanding or creepy and she'd probably been giving him really confusing mixed messages, equal parts determined not to encourage him and absolutely on fire for him and unable to entirely hide that. He hadn't assumed that their hot kiss meant any kind of further permission and he clearly had a sense of humor about her literal flight from it.

"Well," she said practically. "I suppose that this beats having to fake a trip to the ladies' room."

Damned if Tobias didn't look twice as handsome as ever when he grinned at her over the table. He was clean-shaven again.

Candles were lit between them and water was poured, no ice cubes necessary. No one handed them menus.

"I took the liberty of arranging the meal," Tobias said. "I talked to Eva about your favorite dishes and the chef here is a master of Mediterranean food."

Harriet was impressed. He'd gone to great lengths to order her a special meal, with accommodations that both acknowledged her flightiness and made gentle fun of it. It certainly had to come at great trouble and expense.

He was courteous and quick with the server, who was not at all dressed for the weather, and then they were alone on the balcony again.

"Thank you," Harriet said, feeling shy. "This is...really nice."

It was, too. There was quiet music being piped in, and the street sounds were distant over that, muffled in old snow. It was dark, except for the twinkle of the city lights, and the candlelight was moody and romantic. They were served bread that steamed in the cold air, and warmed mulled red wine of a silky high quality.

"I've been looking up those artists you were telling me about," Tobias said, cupping his hands around his wineglass like it was hot chocolate. "Capet and Labille-Guiard. What a saga! How did I not know about them?"

"They were erased," Harriet said in righteous outrage. "History has always been written by men who couldn't bear the idea of skilled, successful women."

Tobias neither agreed ingratiatingly nor denied her heated assessment, but prodded Harriet for more information, and they spoke of technical achievements and undersung scientists, lamenting together over Tesla (the scientist, not the car) and artists of the ages who were the "wrong" colors and genders and religions and orientations.

Tobias was surprisingly educated—he might have crammed on pre-Revolutionary salon art to try to impress her, but his knowledge of other subjects was too broad to brush off as some kind of courtship attempt, and Harriet found herself learning fascinating new tidbits as they talked, filing some to verify later, because he also had a droll sense of humor and Harriet didn't entirely trust that she wasn't being baited.

He had a quick and clever mind, and he wasn't afraid to argue, clearly not trying to appease her when their opinions differed. Harriet thought that she would miss having the conversational advantage of her cleavage to distract him with, covered in winter wear, but she didn't, even once, too caught up in their wordplay.

Their dinner was served almost unnoticed into their conversation, and Harriet was delighted by the flavor. It steamed in the cool air, like their breath, and they ate quickly, continuing their banter long after their plates were cleared.

Dessert was a crème brûlée, crisped by torch at their table, and Harriet was surprised to realize that she was shivering, but had no real desire to leave. She hadn't expected to enjoy their dinner except as a stepping stone to sleeping together, but she couldn't remember when she'd last had so much fun.

"You're cold!" Tobias realized.

There was a pregnant pause, and Harriet knew that he knew that it was the moment for an invitation somewhere warm. This was it. This was his opportunity to ask her to go upstairs with him and she would say yes, with no strings. She wondered briefly if he'd actually planned this, if his playful outdoor dinner had been designed to make inside seem appealing and necessary as a part of his playbook into her pants.

But she didn't think it was, and really, was that worse than her cold-hearted plan to love him and leave him? Harriet knew that the longer she waited for him to be chivalrous, the more likely she was to lose what was left of her heart. "Do you have a room?" she asked suggestively.

CHAPTER 18

obias felt his heart soar.

He hadn't wanted to force the issue, or make another heavy-handed invitation for Harriet to rebuff. She was a wild bird, and he couldn't cage her, no matter how desperate he was to make her his own.

And by his ancestor's underworld, she was everything he'd known she would be. She was sharp-witted and creative, as quick with words as she was on her feet, and she absolutely shone with passion for the topics they spoke on. She was civic-minded, and fierce for justice, but charmingly pedestrian in her love of low humor and cheap media.

He also reminded himself that she was a wanted art thief, and that she'd stolen jewels right out from under his own nose, which was not a minor feat, or a minor sin, in direct conflict with her apparent goodness. She was complicated.

And so was he.

"I have a room," he told her, glad that he'd taken that step. He had not just *a* room, but the *best* room, though he didn't want to brag. She would be able to see that for herself.

They pushed their chairs back, loud on the empty deck,

and put their napkins on the table as they stood. Tobias offered his arm and Harriet put her gloved fingers in the crook of his elbow. He wished he weren't wearing such a heavy coat and could feel the touch of them against his skin. "This way," he said.

He led her back through the crowded restaurant, keenly aware of the speculative looks that they got, and out to the elevators in the lobby. He scanned his keycard to gain access to the penthouse level. Harriet didn't say a word until they arrived at the door to his suite.

Tobias paused before unlocking it. "Harriet," he said hesitantly. He should tell her that he knew about the jewels she'd stolen, about who she *was*. He didn't want secrets between them. He wanted Harriet, raw and whole and his completely.

But she was leaning over to kiss him then, her lips cool and tasting of crème brûlée against his, and nothing else mattered.

He wasn't sure how he got them into the penthouse; his hands were busy finding the buttons of her coat and shucking it off of her so that he could see the slinky dress she was wearing beneath it. She was breathtaking, every curve and sweep of her skin absolutely intoxicating under his fingers. "Harriet," he breathed, and she shuddered as if he'd invoked a spell.

"Tobias," she murmured in return. "Tobias…"

She shimmied out of her coat and her shoes, dropping her height several inches but still towering above him. Tobias flung off his own overcoat and slipped his shoes off without untying them. He never bothered with lifts, though salesmen frequently tried to convince him he needed them. His shirt followed, and he was gratified by Harriet's hiss of appreciation. Gnomes weren't slouches, and he knew that he had a well-formed chest and great shoulders.

It was only fair that she shimmy out of her dress then,

and render *him* speechless—not that they'd been speaking—with her magnificent breasts.

They were just at the height where he could bury his face between them, one of the many unsung advantages to his stature. He kissed each one in turn and cupped them in his hands and pulled her close up against him as he caressed her and teased off her bra.

She whimpered and let him finish undressing her, all of her splendid skin and lanky limbs like a buffet of places to touch and kiss and tease.

They hadn't made it to the bedroom yet, barely inside the sitting room, and one of them must have kicked the door shut behind them.

"Harriet," he tried again, remembering that he wanted to come clean with what he knew about her.

"Shut up and show me to your room," Harriet said, tugging at his belt.

Tobias was happy to comply, dizzy with the smell and feel of her as they staggered through the door into the bedroom.

The broad bed had been scattered with rose petals that bruised as he tipped her back onto the silk comforter. "Harriet," he said again, but he didn't even attempt to follow it with more.

He was hard and helpless to resist her, and when she figured out the clasp of his pants and freed him Tobias had to make a guttural noise of need before he could choke back his own desire and remember to slow down.

He kissed her deeply, whispering, "Patience," as she squirmed and clawed at him, spreading her legs and trying to draw him into her.

"I am not patient," she panted. "I never have been."

"I am," Tobias said. "I am as patient as the earth for the right reward."

Staying slow was still one of the hardest things Tobias

had ever done, she was so eager and willing and he wanted nothing more than to bury himself in her now and forever. But he knew that she was more than a quick release and a one-night pleasure, and if he wanted to win her, really have her, he would have to make it more memorable than a simple desperate tumble. He kissed her sweet, delicious mouth again, and again, then kissed down her neck as he slipped down her, letting his cock trail down her thigh, denying her the penetration she was begging for.

She was so tightly wound that he could feel the muscles in her stomach flexing as he kissed over them, and her hands balled the comforter into her fists when his mouth found the mound of her pleasure. She made helpless noises as he licked her, flicking his tongue between her lips and sucking at her clit.

He played her like an instrument, listening to her music and gauging her desperation until he was sure she was going to crest, then crawled to kiss her with her own juices and plunge into her at last, stealing her cries with his mouth.

*H*arriet was not prudish or inexperienced, but she had honestly not known that she could reach the heights that Tobias showed her.

He prolonged her pleasure exquisitely, slowing just when she would have begged for speed, teasing her and torturing her when she was frantic for release. "Please, please," she said, writhing under his spell, until he was finally filling her and she could say nothing because he was kissing her hard and hot and she was lost in the feeling of his heavy body pressing her down into a state of pure passion.

And he wasn't finished with her then, slowing and relinquishing her mouth to let her catch her breath before he was stroking harder and deeper and she was losing her mind all over again.

She was starting to imagine that he would not ever be done with her, that she would turn into a shell of herself and break into pieces of perfect happiness when he made a noise that was partly her name and partly a prayer and partly a magic spell, his own release an inevitability.

All the beautiful bunchy muscles in his neck and shoulders tensed up and he snapped at the air near her ear as he groaned and thrust and Harriet had one last wave of bliss before they were both falling together.

They cradled together for a long time, arms wrapped around each other as the framework of the world finally stopped moving around them.

This was where Harriet belonged, she thought. Her owl was right. It wasn't just sex, it wasn't just satisfaction, it was this, having Tobias up against her, in her arms and in her heart, crushing her just a little.

"You're crying," he said quietly, rolling to lie beside her with his face so close to hers that Harriet couldn't even quite focus on him. He wiped her traitorous tears tenderly from her cheek.

"I don't know why," she admitted. Then she wondered if she really did, feeling raw and vulnerable. She was crying because this happiness might be hers, she might actually have a chance with this amazing guy who was crazy about her. She was crying because she thought she didn't deserve this kind of joy and fulfillment. She was a liar and a thief, everything about her was false and fake and she could never earn Tobias's big heart if he knew what she really was.

Panic rose up and choked her, but Tobias had his hands on either side of her face now and he was gazing earnestly into her eyes. "I love you," he said, driving the knife of her guilt the rest of the way into her heart.

"You don't know me," Harriet protested. "We only met a few days ago."

"I know you," Tobias said. "I know how smart and sly you are."

Sly? It seemed a two-edged compliment, but Harriet thought that it was probably true. "This isn't love," she said quietly. It couldn't be. *Love* wasn't her destiny.

"I know you," Tobias repeated. "I know that you are a

clever, creative, beautiful woman who challenges me in every way. I know that you are afraid of love, and that you are the bravest and most good-hearted person I've ever met."

How was he so beautiful and sure when he was obviously so *wrong?* If there had been an open window, Harriet would have shifted and flown away right at that very moment, leaving behind her four hundred dollar shoes and her heart.

It took all of her willpower to roll away from Tobias and sit up, crossing her arms over her bare breasts. "You don't know me," she insisted. "If we tried to make this a *thing,* I'd just break your heart."

Tobias snorted and Harriet glanced back to find that he'd sprawled with his arms behind his head, shameless in his gorgeous nudity. "Maybe I'd break *your* heart," he suggested with a grin. "I mean, I think if we're tallying things at this point, you should remember that I gave you three pretty amazing orgasms and I only got one. I know you well enough to know that you won't want to carry a debt."

There was no way that Harriet could not laugh at that, no matter how much she didn't want to. "You are unbelievable! You think I have an…orgasm deficit to pay you?"

"It would haunt you forever," Tobias warned with mock seriousness.

"How would I possibly repay that?"

"You could try not to come," Tobias challenged.

Harriet hated her body's trilling response to the words, remembering how he'd stroked her and her inevitable submission to his talented fingers and mouth. "You're unbelievable," she repeated, scrubbing a hand across her face. Crying after sex like a stupid schoolgirl who still believed in true love. The only debt she had now was for her dignity.

Her dress was in a heap on the floor where Tobias had peeled it off of her, a few steps beyond her coat. Her bra was hanging off the back of a chair. "Look," she said, gathering them up and dressing swiftly, "I don't want to lead you on. This was really hot, but I don't want you thinking I owe you *anything*. Don't turn one night of dirty fun into a fairy tale, hot pants. Those shoes don't fit this princess."

Mate, her owl creeled in confusion.

A mate isn't a mandate, Harriet insisted. *He's better off without us.*

He's a man! We can date! her owl tried to argue absurdly. *Mandate!*

Tobias sat up, but he didn't try to stop her from yanking her clothing back on. "You don't *have* to go," was all that he said, entirely too gently and understanding.

"It's almost midnight," Harriet said. "My carriage is going to turn into a pumpkin." There was no graceful way to put on a bra, so she had to twist around, trying not to give him a gratuitous view.

"Leave me a shoe?" Tobias suggested to her back.

"A four hundred dollar Armani shoe? How good do you think you were?" Harriet demanded.

"It's four hundred dollars for the pair," Tobias corrected her. "It's always worth less when you break up a matched set."

Harriet wondered if his statement didn't sound slightly pointed. She suspected that he was trying to hint at something, but the side zipper on her dress was proving complicated and she was concentrating most of her attention on not damaging Eva's careful stitching.

"Harriet," Tobias started.

He was going to beg her to stay and Harriet knew that she was too weak to say no. She wanted nothing more than to crawl back in that big bed with him and let him murmur sweet nothings that she might even believe until they both fell asleep.

"You were great," Harriet said breezily as she finally

mastered the zipper and pulled her coat on over herself like a cloak of not-caring. "Don't let it go to your head or anything, but this was super fun, sweet lips." There was no point in denying that she'd enjoyed herself. "Five stars. Would recommend."

"Harriet," Tobias said again, more dangerously yet.

"Don't get clingy," Harriet warned him. "I'll dock you stars and ruin your rating."

"Your stars are the only ones that matter," Tobias said gravely.

But Harriet's stars were seriously crossed, and if she stayed, she knew that she'd have nothing but aching regret, no matter how her owl was fighting her and insisting that they stay. "Miss me!" she sang, slipping into her shoes and marching out the door.

She had to go all the way to the ground floor to find a door that opened to the outdoors, keenly aware of her sticky, rumpled state, and as soon as she was free of the building, she flung herself into the sky.

The city bell tower was striking midnight as she flew to the condo that didn't feel like a home.

CHAPTER 20

Tobias let himself fall back on the bed. It smelled like smashed rose petals and sex.

He had badly overplayed his hand and used entirely the wrong cards. He'd been desperate to make her stop crying and making people laugh was always the first tool he had in his toolbox. Well, the second to the *obvious* tool.

And for one moment, he thought it might work. He'd surprised her into laughing, and from there, he thought he could coax her back to happiness and keep her close.

But she'd gone straight from laughter to flight, and he was left with empty hands again.

He should have just told her that she was the only woman he'd ever met that he could imagine spending his life with. He should have told her that he knew about her childhood and history of crime…and charity. He should have told her what *he* was, and how important she was to him.

But he feared that being honest would terrify her. Behind all of her bravado and cleverness, she was afraid. *I'd break your heart,* she said plaintively. She wasn't worried about *her* heart because she didn't know she had one, and if Tobias tried to show it to her, she would never believe it.

He took an efficient shower in the gleaming master bathroom and wrapped himself in the hotel robe, rolling up the sleeves. He fished his cellphone from his pants pocket and stared at the screen. He was pretty sure that an immediate text would only result in being blocked.

Tobias was very good at everything that he did, and a big part of becoming good at things was skipping the time-wasting steps where he tried everything wrong. He learned business by asking successful businessmen shrewd questions. He learned manufacturing by touring the plants of the companies that dominated the markets and taking notes. He learned finances by studying rich people—the quietly rich, not the noisy ones trying to impress people. He never assumed that he'd prosper by finding things out the hard way. If he wanted a new skillset, he went to an expert directly and cut out the steep learning curve.

And if he wanted lessons on courtship, he knew just who to call…and it would be mid-morning in Norway already.

"Underhills," the voice at the other end of the line sang out.

"Hey, squirt, put Grandma on. Tell her it's important."

"I'm not a squirt, you're a squirt," his nephew protested. "Grandma! It's Uncle Tobias!"

There was the rustle of a passing phone that was apparently nearly fumbled into the sink. "I'm in the middle of making julekake, darling, what do you need?"

Tobias had a stab of homesickness. Norwegian yule cake, fondly called jewel cake, was a favorite holiday treat, like a better, fluffy fruitcake, with candied fruit like jewels throughout. He loved to eat it warm from the oven, spread with melting butter.

But it wasn't the Christmas bread that he actually wanted,

it was a home, and he wanted Harriet in that home. "I need to know how to win someone who doesn't want to be won," he said bluntly.

The phone really was dropped then, though fortunately not into the sink, and there was a chaos of noise that was followed at last by the slamming of a door and his mother's quiet, hopeful voice. "You met someone?"

"More than just someone," he confessed. More than just *met*. He was not sure if he would ever be able to erase the memory of her surrender to him, the feel of her hungry mouth, the flutter of her heartbeat under his lips when he kissed her neck.

"Oh, Tobias, I'm so happy to hear that!" Was his mother *crying*? What was it with bringing women to tears today?

"It's complicated," he warned. "She doesn't want anything serious."

"Oh, honey, women always say that. I certainly said that to your father."

"I don't want to be that jerk who can't take a no," Tobias said frankly.

His mother chuckled. "Of course you don't, darling. I raised you right. But it can be a little terrifying to give up your heart, and an independent woman worth having is going to put up a fight at first. You stay respectful and be a gentleman, and she'll come around. The Underhills always win their wars."

"Is that what Dad did with you?"

"Not at all," his mother said frankly. "He kidnapped me from a party, punched a man twice his height who called me a whore, and then fell down a flight of stairs and broke his leg. I spent two nights with him at the hospital and we scandalized the nurses."

Tobias pinched the bridge of his nose. "I don't think that's a good game plan with Harriet."

"I'm not really suggesting it. If the timer is going off, check the julekake!" she hollered. "Make sure it's not burning and if it's hollow-sounding, take it out! Now, Tobias, tell me about this woman who's stolen your heart. Does she know about gnomes?"

"I don't think she entirely *believes* in gnomes," Tobias said. "But she's a shifter. A snowy owl shifter."

"I certainly didn't believe in gnomes before I met your father," his mother agreed. "Is she from a good family?"

"She's an orphan," Tobias said. "Abandoned at birth. She went through the foster system."

"Oh, Tobias!" Tobias realized that he could actually hear his mother's heart melting. "No wonder she's afraid of a relationship. The poor motherless thing! Can you bring her here for Christmas?"

The idea of Harriet in his mother's kitchen was equal parts horrifying and deeply appealing. "I don't think she'd come," he admitted.

"Oh, posh. Everyone wants a home to go to for Christmas. Give me her number, darling and I will call her myself."

"That is *not* why I called you," Tobias protested. He was not going to let his mother make his moves *for* him.

"Well, maybe you're too threatening," his mother said sensibly. "You do have a very forceful personality. I could certainly smooth the way..."

"Absolutely not," Tobias snarled.

"See, there you go, being all forceful. There's no reason to get upset with me." His mother, for all of her good qualities, was masterful at shifting the blame.

"Mom..."

"Here's what you should do, darling..."

CHAPTER 21

*H*arriet showered ferociously, trying to scrub off the memory of Tobias's touches.

Her plan to take the edge off her owl's foolish mate obsession by sleeping with him had backfired spectacularly, because now she knew exactly what she wouldn't be getting, and she'd never be able to match the happiness she'd briefly allowed herself.

Her owl sulked, confused by Harriet's flight and frustrated by her reluctance to stay where they obviously belonged.

*Because we **don't** belong there,* Harriet said, not sure if she was trying to assure herself or her owl of the fact.

We don't, her owl agreed unexpectedly. *We belong in his nest.*

Gnomes don't have nests, Harriet scoffed.

Gnest, then, her owl retorted.

Harriet had not realized that her owl could grasp humor at that level and snorted a laugh despite herself. She sobered, thinking wistfully of a nest—of a *home*—with Tobias. Waking up with him, breakfast across from him, making cozy domestic decisions together.

She tipped her head up into the water. This shower was not cold enough to do its job, and her soap was too *soft*.

How did she think that could possibly work? Did she involve him in her life of crime? Would she coordinate heists with him? How did taxes work then? Married, filing fraudulently?

Married? Her owl chirped in delight.

Harriet cursed herself for letting her mind wander so far. She was not going to *marry* Tobias. That was not her destiny.

She turned the water off and stood while it cooled on her skin before she reached for a towel and wrapped herself up with a sigh. How could it be that she was hungry for Tobias all over again? He'd just released all of her tensions in ways that she hadn't even known were possible and she was thinking about him, desperate for his touch already.

That's all this was, she told herself. Passing obsession. If it was a place in her brain that she could scoop out with a spoon, she'd be opening her skull with a can opener right now.

She dried off efficiently and slipped into a pair of fleece pajamas, trying to soothe her owl with promises of flying and hunting, very soon.

Her owl only sulked, unhappy with Harriet's lack of cooperation.

SHE BLOCKED his number four times over the next three days, breaking down and unblocking it a few hours later. He didn't text, and Harriet hated herself for wishing he would. She started five of her own texts, but what would she say?

I want to do that again.

I don't want to ever see you again.
I can't stop thinking about you.
I screwed up.
You don't know me.

She deleted every word of them, hoped he hadn't seen the teasing three dots, scolded herself for even thinking he *might*, blocked him again, and promptly unblocked him.

She went to the senator's holiday ball, caught herself getting excited at the sight of a short figure with long blond hair who turned out to be the senator's daughter and took herself home in a huff, having stolen exactly nothing.

Her owl was confused and puzzled and a miserable companion, vacillating between scolding her and moping like an oil-soaked duck.

You're a drama queen, Harriet told her. *We don't need a mate.*

Tobias, Tobias, Tobias, more TACOS.

You're disgusting and I'm going to hork up a pellet if you keep cooing over him.

But she couldn't blame all of her obsession on her owl. Even when the flying fuzzball was quiet and sulky, Harriet was the one thinking about Tobias, about his dark eyes and his flashing grin. She was the one remembering his fingers on her flesh, the way he'd made her weak with longing and whole with surrender.

When his text finally came through, she stared at it in longing and confusion.

I want to make a trade.

There was no eggplant emoji to make it clear what he was looking to trade and Harriet could not imagine what else he would want from her.

Tobias was beginning to think that Harriet wasn't going to show up at all.

There had been no reply to his first text, though it showed that it had been viewed, and the second text still sat in unread limbo. Had she blocked him?

Tobias rubbed his arms, trying to move blood back into them. It was considerably colder than it had been on the night of their balcony dinner date, the sky slate gray and threatening snow. He was going to freeze to death on the roof of Harriet's bakery, and Frank and Bruno would probably slap a pointed hat on him and put his frozen body in someone's garden as a joke.

Just as he was prepared to call for an extraction, he heard a little *who* and turned to find that Harriet had flown silently out of the sky and was sitting as a snowy owl on the parapet.

Even as an owl she was gorgeous, fluffy and silvery white with scattered dark banding. Her golden eyes were unwavering above a wicked beak. As he watched, she stepped forward off the edge of the roof with her feathered claws and flowed into her human form, smartly dressed in a long wool coat and fur-trimmed white hat.

"How did you get on my roof?" she demanded.

"Helicopter," Tobias said with a shrug. "I know you like open places and thought you would appreciate the home space advantage."

"You've redecorated," she observed. There was a table set for two, with an embroidered ivory table cloth.

Tobias had directed his crew to shovel away the snow and hang sparkling Christmas lights around the space, stringing them from the communications tower and power lines, anywhere that they would reach.

"Well, it was a little spartan," Tobias said. "The wine is probably frozen, sorry, and the cheddar bread balls are cold. I didn't expect you to take so long getting here."

"Sorry, Martha Stewart. I had other business to attend to."

Then Harriet saw what lay on the table before him and all of the color left her cheeks as her gaze flashed up to his in alarm and dismay.

It was the pair to the bracelet that she'd stolen, just a week before.

Tobias feared that she was going to turn and flee before she heard him out. She was poised to leap into the air and she glanced to the side like she was looking to see if he was springing a trap on her. Her breath steamed in the cold air, fast and close to panic.

"I know," he said as calmly as he could manage, leaving his hands loose on the table. "I know that you stole the other one. I know that you stole Victoria Henning's emerald necklace at the RRTA's art auction last year. And I suspect you might have had something to do with the missing Monet painting from the private collection of Doctor Stenbegger a few years back."

"What are you going to do about it, Nancy Drew?" Harriet challenged. "Turn me in for a reward?"

"You can't think that I need money," Tobias scoffed. "I bought the other bracelet outright, for the full price of the pair."

"What do you want then?" she asked, her voice hard. "Is this just about…conquest?"

"Harriet, I have frozen my balls off for you twice now, and protected you from investigation and paid off the people looking for you, and I have even *called my mother.* If I just wanted sex, I could get any woman I wanted in my bed with a fraction of the hassle and far less frostbite."

"Maybe you just like the unobtainable ones," she countered.

"Maybe I just like *you.*"

Harriet had no answer for that, her breath continuing to steam in the cold air in jerky puffs.

"Maybe I just *love* you," Tobias said gently. "Maybe you're exactly the kind of amazing partner that I've always wanted in my life."

"I'm a liar and a thief," Harriet reminded him, backing away.

"Maybe, but you're an honest liar and a noble thief," Tobias said. "You do what you think is right and help people that you think deserve it."

"You…don't know me." Harriet turned away and went to the edge of the roof and stood at the parapet. Tobias was afraid for a moment that she was going to jump off and fly away, but she paused there. "You…don't know me," she repeated, turning away.

"I *want* to know you," Tobias said, rising to his feet. He approached her slowly, not wanting to scare her into bolting away. "I want to know everything about you. I want to know why you don't like potato chips and what your favorite music is. I want to know where you're ticklish, and what kind of pets you like. I want to know why you save misfits and pretend you don't care about them."

He was close enough to touch her now, and to hear her quiet words. "I'm not worth *knowing.*"

"I want to know who made you think that and find them and knock them into a pit of biting red ants," Tobias said fiercely. "Followed by a sandpaper scrub and a hot alcohol bath."

"Remind me not to piss you off," Harriet said with a chuckle. "That's a pretty graphic threat for a Christmas elf."

Tobias closed the distance between them and slowly wrapped his arms around her waist, leaning his head in the small of her back. "You bring out the ferocious alpha gnome in me."

She slowly melted in his embrace.

"You're warm, but I'm freezing my nads off," Tobias pointed out after a moment, and he felt Harriet's laughter through her entire frame.

After a moment, she squirmed free of his arms and Tobias prepared to let her reluctantly go, sure this was her moment of flight after all. Instead, she turned and sat down on the parapet facing him like the strength had gone out of her legs. Tobias stepped closer, between her knees and she drew him into her arms, leaning her head against his.

"You said you wanted to trade," she said in quiet surrender. "You have all of my dirty secrets, what else did you want from me?"

"It's only fair that you know my mysteries, too," Tobias said, unable to resist kissing her cheek. "I am a gnome, from a long and noble line of them."

She backed away far enough that she could give him a skeptical look. "I know you say that. That's not a secret, but what does it mean? Besides very unpredictable facial hair, apparently?" She tugged at his stubble. "Honestly, how many times a day do you shave to keep it under control?"

"A few, if I'm going for a kissably clean jaw," Tobias confessed.

She seemed to take that as a challenge and she kissed his cheek and nuzzled against it. "Mmm, I could get used to that. What else does it mean? Will you clean my house for me? Make me shoes?"

"That's house elves," Tobias snorted. "Totally different family. Gnomes have much more impressive skills."

"Very modest of you, Casanova." It was starting to snow, big, fat flakes that settled on her hat and went invisible in the white fur.

Tobias grinned and caught her ear in his teeth, loving how it made her breath hiss in her mouth. "Those weren't the skills I meant, though they should certainly not be discounted. We have to go downstairs so I can show you."

"There's a pull-out couch in my office, but didn't you just say that those weren't the skills you meant?"

"A little further downstairs," Tobias said.

"We should probably have a frank talk about what kind of downstairs permissions you think you're getting now," Harriet said.

"I'm not going to need any permissions if I frostbite my fun stuff before I can use it," Tobias pointed out.

CHAPTER 23

*H*arriet punched the code into the security panel at the roof entrance and went with Tobias down the stairs, hand in hand. She was glad that Eva was out for the day, though she wasn't sure where the young woman had gone. They stopped at the second floor landing, and Harriet was quite prepared to take him to her office, but he pulled her further down the stairs. "We have to go to the kitchen."

"Kinky!" Harriet said, but she was wild with curiosity now. She had genuinely thought that Tobias was only teasing when he implied that it wasn't his bedroom talents that he intended to show her.

They did pause at the next stair landing to kiss, and Harriet thought that she would never tire of the feel of his body up against hers, strong and sexy. He was definitely —*obviously*—interested in pursuing sheet shimmies with her, whatever else he had to reveal, and the cold had apparently not had a lasting impact on his self-proclaimed *fun stuff*.

He broke off their kiss at last and led her down into the bakery and back into the stainless steel kitchen.

"I need sugar," he said, gazing around.

"I just offered you that," Harriet said with a chuckle, going to the cabinet where they kept the big covered barrel of sugar.

"That might be a second course," Tobias said with a wink. He used the scoop to pour a scant handful of sugar into one palm.

"Is this going to be hygienic?" Harriet had to ask. She could not imagine what he was going to do with it.

"Give me just a moment," Tobias said. He dropped the scoop back into the barrel and worked his hands together, looking a bit like a gymnast chalking his hands, or an artist shaping a small clay ball.

Harriet was watching Tobias's face as he concentrated on his mysterious handful of sugar. For once, he wasn't looking at her, all of his attention on his hands, and she could drink in his features.

He was so handsome and dangerously dear to her. It wasn't just his compactly-built body that turned her on, but the feeling that hid in his eyebrows, and the laugh lines around his eyes. It was the planes of his face, and the angles of his nose, and his eyes, with those long lashes and green depths.

It was the way he *got* her, and how desperately she craved that understanding, even more than his touch.

He was turning a little red now, clearly exerting himself even though he wasn't moving at all, and Harriet marveled at the color in his cheeks and at the tip of his nose. Then he sucked his breath in and uncupped his hands.

Water dripped from them.

At first, Harriet thought that his bizarre exertion had made his palms sweat, but then she saw what else was in his hands.

"Did you know that sugar is made up of hydrogen,

oxygen, and carbon?" he asked, panting slightly. "I can turn it to water and…"

"Diamond," Harriet said in awe.

It was a raw diamond, not cut, but Harriet knew her gems. It was a lump of unassuming carbon in its strongest crystal form, catching the light from its multiple facets. It wasn't that large, five or six carats at the most, but it was one of the most flawless raw stones that Harriet had ever seen. It was perfectly clear, which made sense, since color and flaws were usually due to mineral inclusions, and Tobias had just made it out of pure elements.

"It's not cut," he said, wiping his palms on his thighs one by one as he looked at the stone critically in the light. "That's part of the value of a diamond, of course, but I know a jeweler who does that work." He was still breathing hard, but the high color was starting to fade from his face. "You probably do, too."

"It's probably worth three thousand dollars, even uncut," Harriet said in awe as he dropped it into her hands. "And you just made it from a few pennies worth of sugar."

"There's a limit to how often I can do it," Tobias said with the deliberate shrug that Harriet was beginning to realize meant he was actually embarrassed. "And it does no good to flood the market, of course. Why are you looking at me like that?"

"I did not realize that you could get hotter," Harriet was startled enough to admit. "And then you did."

His flashing grin struck straight past all her armor, deep into her heart and she had to ask, haltingly, "Do gnomes have mates?"

His grin didn't falter, but it did soften. "No," he said, confirming her suspicion. "Not like shifters do." Then he added, "But we know a good thing when we see it."

Harriet wanted to drag her gaze away. She wasn't a good

thing. There wasn't anything good about her. The raw diamond in her hand felt like a lead weight.

"Harriet, am I your mate?" Tobias's voice was so gentle, but so firm. He wasn't going to let her get away without answering him.

This was Harriet's chance to do what she did best: lie. Tobias didn't know for sure, and she could tell him now that this was nothing more than attraction and diversion. She could shrug this thing between them off like it meant nothing,

He guessed, but he didn't know, and if she told him that he wasn't her mate, she could rip herself free of him like an old Band-Aid and...and...

Harriet didn't need her owl to prompt her to answer.

She was tired of lies, of working alone, of constantly shielding her heart. She wanted what Tobias was offering with open arms. She wanted it so badly and it scared her so much.

And she wasn't going to let fear decide her fate.

"You're my mate," she confessed.

CHAPTER 24

Tobias felt like he'd just been handed a live snake or a hand grenade with no pin.

He *was* her mate.

He'd hoped so hard that for a moment it was deeply unreal, the words that he'd imagined her saying, that he'd longed to hear.

"Don't be ringing any wedding bells," Harriet said tartly, breaking the spell. "Just because my owl thinks you hung the moon doesn't mean that I'm interested in nailing my wings to any man, gorgeous diamond-making gnome or not."

"You have to admit it's an impressive skill," Tobias said slyly. "And I am *very* marriageable quality. I've been *Time Magazine's* number one most eligible bachelor four times now."

Harriet still had the diamond in her hand and she tossed it lightly. "Your ego really is one of your greatest attributes," she said with a shake of her head "And you might be marriageable quality if I were the marrying type. But I am just not the sort of woman you bring home to your mother."

Tobias snapped his fingers. "Which reminds me that you

are invited to my mother's for Christmas this year. I already have the plane tickets. We leave Sunday morning."

"Were you planning to ask me? Or were you going to break into my house and kidnap me?" Tobias thought her outrage sounded softened with humor.

"Kidnapping was on the table," he admitted. "There's some successful family history of it. But I also had a great deal of dirt on you that I thought I could probably use for leverage."

"You planned to *blackmail* me into going to your mother's?"

"I had decided not to," Tobias said magnanimously. "I figured I'd cash in your orgasm debt instead."

"I do not owe you orgasms!"

"One of your best qualities is your intense sense of fair play," Tobias said confidently. "I've done a lot of research on you and I know you a little by now. You couldn't just let me get away with giving you more fun than I got."

"Couldn't I?" Harriet challenged. "Would you like to find out?"

Tobias bared his teeth at her and growled, "Your home or mine?"

She hesitated and Tobias wondered if he'd pushed too fast. He might be her mate, but she was still understandably cautious. He knew that it would be a long and careful courtship, that he'd have to tame her slowly to get her to trust him completely. "Neutral ground?" he suggested. "You said there was a pull-out couch…"

He wasn't sure if it was the appeal of a place that wasn't conceding to his home or opening hers to him, or if, when she kissed him, that she was only desperate for something closer. Tobias drew her up the carpeted stairs and into her office. They did not actually get the couch pulled out, but it was a roomy piece of furniture and there was plenty of space on the cushions to play out their challenge, and plenty of positions that they hadn't made it through during their previous night together.

He coaxed even more pleasure from her this time, having cataloged what she liked best, where she liked to be touched, how to tease her to breaking…

And break she did, crying out in sweet bliss that drove him to his own release.

"Who won?" he asked, when he could.

"Who *didn't* win?" she asked, almost purring in contentment beneath him.

He cradled her in his arms, so satisfied and glad to have her there, so happy to have a hope of keeping her there forever that he didn't even care where they were.

Harriet Slade was definitely a challenge.

One that he was up for…in every way.

CHAPTER 25

*H*arriet had faced down mob bosses and pulled off impossible heists. She had challenged some of the dirtiest characters in the underworld, and been involved in ugly barroom brawls as an underaged brat without flinching or fleeing.

Nothing had ever terrified her like this mission.

"Uncle Tobias!"

The white door to the picturesque red house was flung open and a short-legged form dashed out like a two-legged puppy to attach itself to Tobias's waist. A second followed it, shrieking the same thing.

Harriet stood aside and let them pull Tobias inside out of the snow, following them with their luggage—a full set of matching leather pieces that had been a gift from Tobias. She wondered if he knew exactly what it had meant to her, as a foundling child being passed from foster to foster with nothing better than trash bags for all of her earthly possessions. She suspected he did, but he only shrugged and pointed out that bribery was a step above kidnapping and blackmail.

Harriet latched the door carefully behind her and gazed around in ill-concealed awe. Outside had been holiday card perfection, with snow-covered mountains and darling Christmas-lit houses clustered by the open water's edge. Inside was warmth and the smell of spices and pine, all the light golden and cozy. She was dazzled most by the press of people, shouting greetings, only half of them in English. She wasn't sure which ones were gnome-short and which were young, there was such a press of them, from squalling toddlers to gray-haired elders. She met uncles and cousins and siblings in a dizzying array.

"You must be Harriet!"

"Mrs. Underhill," she said politely to the woman who parted the crowd, not letting a tiny part of her uncertainty show. "Thank you for your hospitality."

To her alarm, the woman pulled Harriet forward and folded her into an irresistible embrace. "Darling!" she said. "We are so happy to have Tobias's mate with us for Christmas. You must be a saint to put up with him."

Tobias gave a good-natured laugh. "Thank you, Mother! It is lovely to see you, too." He gave her a kiss on her cheek.

"I…thought gnomes didn't have mates," Harriet said quietly. She gave Tobias a sour look. She was barely used to the idea herself and wasn't sure if she liked him being so free about the term.

"Just because they don't have mates doesn't mean they can't *be* mates," Mrs. Underhill pointed out with irrefutable logic. "Now take off your coat and let the kids show you up to your room. Tobias, keep your fingers out of the food. You might be a bigshot CEO in America, but that doesn't mean you can act like you were raised in a barn here. Dinner is an hour and you are a grown gnome who can wait to eat with the rest of us."

That said, she slipped Harriet a sugar cookie and pushed

her towards the back of the house. "I know that you're both *very* tired from your long journey."

They were escorted by three chortling children up two flights of narrow stairs to a tiny bedroom. Harriet had to duck into the doorway as Tobias chased his nieces and nephews away with threats of tossing them into the fjord if they touched his things.

"There's only one bed," Harriet observed, putting her bags down inside the door. She was still holding the sugar cookie. The roof sloped down to a dormer that looked out over the water to the mountains beyond. Distant lights sparkled on the opposite shore.

"Mother isn't subtle," Tobias said apologetically. "There isn't a hotel in town, or I'd have spared you this. The population is about a hundred people, a dozen gnomes, and five hundred goats. Not much of a tourist destination. Is that a problem? I'm sorry if they are too much."

He said it like he might simply have a hotel built for her, or call in a helicopter and whisk her away to Oslo. And maybe he could. After all, he could make diamonds with his bare hands and a scoop of sugar.

Harriet sank down onto the bed as Tobias wrestled their bags into the tiny closet and took a bite of the cookie.

"Is this what you picture when you think of a home?" Harriet said wistfully. It wasn't what she had in mind when Tobias had said he was taking her home for Christmas. She'd been thinking high rises and stark white Christmas trees…a New York condo, maybe, or a penthouse.

This was so much better.

"This was the home I grew up in," Tobias said, coming to sit on the bed next to her. Their faces were nearly level when they were sitting together, and it was easy to lean forward and kiss him casually.

He kissed her back, less casually.

"Your mother and half the non-goat population of town are downstairs," she reminded him, feeling shy.

"We're *very* tired from traveling," Tobias reminded her suggestively. "And dinner isn't for an hour…"

Harriet wasn't too tired at all, and Tobias knew by now exactly how to unwind her. There was a tiny attached bathroom and she took a brief shower afterwards and changed into fresh clothes, feeling more able to face the sea of strangers below. She'd never wanted to impress people before, and she wasn't entirely sure which of her selves she ought to be. Tobias, in an embroidered Christmas vest more ridiculous than his beard and belled shoes had been when they met, looked completely at ease.

How was it possible that she was someone he wanted to show off to his family?

"What happens after this?" she wanted to know, hesitating as Tobias opened the door to go down to dinner.

"After dinner?" Tobias asked. "There's the one bed…"

"After Christmas. After this trip. When we go back to River Rock. When we go…home."

Tobias shut the door and returned to sit on the bed next to her.

"Do I give up my unsavory second occupation? Do we get…married? Kids? Pets? Joint checking accounts? Do we buy a house together?"

"What do you picture as home?" Tobias asked.

Harriet shrugged. "I don't know," she admitted. "I didn't have a home growing up." She'd thought that owning a place to call her own was good enough, but now she knew better.

Tobias was looking at her the way that he did, his dark eyes full of compassion and understanding. "A condo, a penthouse, somewhere in between? A suburban townhouse? A place with a yard? Do you want a rorbuer, a fishing cabin on the Norwegian coast? Maybe we build something from scratch. Harriet, I don't care where we are, or what walls are around us. Wherever you are, that's home, that's where I belong."

Gnest, Harriet's owl said, in perfect contentment.

Harriet felt tears prick her eyes. How was it possible to deserve this?

Tobias stepped close and gathered her into his arms, laying his head against her chest and holding her tight against him. "What's wrong?" he asked.

"It's no matter," she said. "I'm just being jet-lagged and emotional."

"If it's g-nome matter," Tobias said slyly, pronouncing the g distinctly, "then it's distinctly my business."

Harriet had to giggle and embrace him in return. "Terrible puns must be why my owl loves you so much," she said.

Still nestled in her cleavage, Tobias tipped his head to look plaintively up at her. "Just your owl, then?"

Harriet gathered her courage. "Not just my owl," she said softly. When his eyes lit up with hope, she added bravely, "I love you, Tobias."

Because she did.

It wasn't just her owl's base instinct that he was their destiny, it was the way that he made her feel like a better person, like a whole person. It was the way that he supported her without judgment, and held the same values that she did. It was the way he looked at her with desire and respect, the way he wanted to show her off but never acted like he owned her. It was the way that she felt whenever she saw him after they were apart.

Like she was coming home.

Gnome sweet gnome.

"Will you marry me?" he asked. "Wait, wait."

He let go of her and dashed back to the bedside table where her half-eaten cookie had been abandoned. Harriet laughed, knowing exactly what he was going to do before he scraped the sugar off the top and held it tight in his hands. It was less sugar than his first demonstration, and took measurably less exertion, but it was still a several carat diamond that lay in his wet hand afterward. "I'll have it cut and set in a ring for you," he promised.

"No," Harriet said, taking the little gem and holding it up to the light above. There must have been other ingredients in the sugar he'd used, because it had a few shots of color and some tiny inclusions.

"No, you won't marry me?" Tobias looked uncharacteristically uncertain.

"Don't have it cut," she said. "You made it exactly like this, and it's like me. Raw, unpolished, a little imperfect. That's what you're marrying."

His eyes crinkled into delight and happiness. "You're saying yes?"

"I'm not saying g-no," Harriet teased him.

Then he was catching her up in his strong arms again and kissing her, and it was all, entirely yes.

She was his, forever, and he was hers. And she would never be alone again.

EPILOGUE

*E*va hesitated at the door. She knew that Harriet was out of the country, but it still felt very weird and wrong to snoop in her office. Harriet had never been anything but kind and generous with Eva, hiring her despite her non-existent credentials and then setting her up with everything she needed to pursue her wild dream of being a fancy dress designer, even if her job title was technically Harriet's assistant.

Harriet had even promised to set Eva up with her own shop, once they had drummed up enough interest in her fanciful designs. Eva wasn't sure she wanted her own shop. She didn't enjoy dealing with people, only in fabric, and she dreaded having to make decisions.

Like this one.

Eva steeled herself and went in. She knew the secret nook under Harriet's desk where she kept the key to the filing cabinet, and she went at once to the right drawer. Behind the files, underneath a few empty folders, was a black velvet bag, and out of it spilled a handful of cut diamonds, emeralds, and rubies.

It was enough to buy out the debt hanging over her head.

Was it enough to cover the cost of her soul? With trembling fingers, Eva dialed the number on her phone.

"Antonio, I need some more information…"

BRUNO LOVED the period between Christmas and New Years because Frank insisted that everyone get paid time off to spend with family. The floor of the factory was quiet and empty and Bruno could use any of the equipment that he wanted without following pesky OSHA rules…like no bears on the line.

He could work at all the odd hours he wanted, with no one hovering over him asking questions. Tobias always wanted to know how they were going to market the things and Frank was there for the pure art of Bruno's work.

Bruno just wanted to be alone and make the shapes that came into his mind—big, elegant shapes that he could only form with the strength of his bear.

The final birdbaths would be poured from a mold, but Bruno relished the brute force it took to make the original forms, swinging specially-made hammers and absorbing the music of the metal as it groaned in submission.

He was glad that Frank and Tobias were off with their mates, because otherwise he would be dragged off to join their holiday revelries and all that he wanted was the peace and quiet and a certain amount of uninterrupted creation time.

Yes, this quiet stretch on the factory floor was exactly what Bruno was looking forward to, and he could not figure out why his bear was stirring restlessly inside of him.

Food? he suggested. His bear tended to be pretty single-minded about basic needs, and otherwise very uncomplicated.

His bear snuffled, unsatisfied with the idea of eating, but still curiously *hungry...*

MARGO WAS NO DUMMY.

She knew that it was easy to underestimate her brain because of her impressive brawn, and she used that shamelessly to avoid conversations that she didn't want to have.

Margo was also no slouch when it came to reading people. She knew when they were trouble, and when they were good people underneath unexpected prickles, like Harriet. No one had to tell her that her bakery boss's business had a seamy underbelly, and it didn't take a lot of quiet observation to figure out Harriet's real purpose. And no one had to tell her how good Tobias was for Harriet.

She'd been hurt at first when Harriet confided in Eva instead of Margo, but she'd carefully let no sign of it show on her face or in her work. It had taken her a long time to realize that part of her jealousy was that she wanted Eva's adoration for herself, and that was something that she hid even more obsessively.

She looked up the stairs now, past the chain that separated Harriet's private business from her public one, listening for Eva's music. She could never tell Eva how she felt because she knew that the pixie young woman didn't have any interest in a literal monster like her.

She was no dummy.

A NOTE FROM ELVA BIRCH

I am absolutely not writing the next book with Margo and Bruno and Eva. That would be absurd. Flamingos are one thing. Gnomes are quite another. But a steamy threesome involving a bear shifter and...? Well, I don't want to spoil their secrets and you should certainly not subscribe to my newsletter or join my Reader's Retreat on Facebook in order to get sneak previews and snippets of this next book that I'm not actually writing...

Your reviews are very much appreciated; I read them all and they help other readers decide whether or not to buy my books! A huge thank you to all of my fabulous beta readers and copy editors; any errors that remain are entirely my own. If you find typos — or you'd just like share your thoughts with me! — please feel free to email me at elvaher self@elvabirch.com.

To find out about my new releases, you can follow me on Amazon, subscribe to my newsletter, or like me on Facebook. Join my Reader's Retreat on Facebook for sneak previews and cut scenes. Find all the links at my webpage: elvabirch.com

I also write under other pen names—keep reading for information about my other available titles...

MORE BY ELVA BIRCH

A Day Care for Shifters: A hot new full-length series about adorable shifter kids and their struggling single parents in a town full of mystery and surprise. Start the series with Wolf's Instinct, when Addison comes to Nickel City to take a job at a very special day care and finds a family to belong to. A gentle ice-cream-straight-from-the-container escape. Sweet and sizzling!

The Royal Dragons of Alaska: A fascinating alternate world where Alaska is ruled by secret dragon shifters. Adventure, romance, and humor! Reluctant royalty, relentless enemies… dogs, camping, and magic! Start with The Dragon Prince of Alaska.

Suddenly Shifters: A hilarious series of novellas, serials, and shorts set in the small town of Anders Canyon, where something (in the water?) is making ordinary citizens turn into shifters. Start with Something in the Water! Also available in audio!

The Flamingo's Fated Mate: It was supposed to be an April Fool's joke, but turned into a sweet-hot, side-splitting romance romp. It certainly won't be a series. I'm definitely not writing a sequel. (If you want sneak previews of the sequel I'm *definitely* not writing, join my Reader's Retreat on Facebook or sign up for my newsletter at elvabirch.com!)

Birch Hearts: An enchanting collection of short stories and novellas. Unconstrained by theme or setting, each short read has romance, magic, and heart, with a satisfying conclusion. And always, the impossible and irresistible. Start with a sampler plate in Prompted 2 for fourteen pieces of sweet-to-sizzling flash fiction, or dive in with the novella, Better Half. Breakup is a free story!

WRITING AS ZOE CHANT

Shifting Sands Resort: A complete ten-book series - plus two collections of shorts. This is a sizzling shifter romance set at a tropical island resort. Each book stands alone but connects into a great mystery with a thrilling conclusion. Start with Tropical Tiger Spy or dive in to the Omnibus edition, with all of the novels, short stories, and novellas in my preferred reading order! Shifting Sands Resort crosses over with **Shifter Kingdom** and **Fire and Rescue Shifters**.

Fae Shifter Knights: A complete four-book fantasy portal romp, with cute pets and swoon-worthy knights stuck in a world of wonders like refrigerators and ham sandwiches. Start with Dragon of Glass!

Green Valley Shifters: A sweet, small town series with single dads, secret shifters, sweet kids, and spinsters. Lowperil and steamy! Standalone books where you can revisit your favorite characters - this series is also complete! Start with Dancing Barefoot! Green Valley Shifters crosses over with **Virtue Shifters**. Start with Timber Wolf!

A PREVIEW OF TROPICAL
TIGER SPY

When Amber booked her vacation at Shifting Sands Resort, she was expecting a lazy tropical vacation at a luxury escape for shifters...she wasn't expecting to meet a sexy under-cover tiger shifter spy who set her blood on fire, or to become a part of his investigation into why shifters are disappearing from the resort! An excerpt of Tropical Tiger Spy.

Amber walked meekly with the guards, trying not to be too obvious about looking around. The dog-catcher was lying unexpectedly loose at her shoulders, and when she glanced at the man holding the pole, he glared back and fingered a button on the handle. The other guard, walking behind her with the gun trained on her, cleared his throat, and Amber put her head down and continued to shamble with them. She was short, so it was easy to walk slowly and look like she was using a normal pace.

The looseness of the noose around her neck got her brain spinning.

They were expecting a mountain cat—an American

mountain cat. A *big* mountain cat. If she shifted, the dog-catcher would be tight around the neck of a big cat. But around her small Andean mountain cat form...

As quickly as the idea occurred to her, Amber put it in motion, shifting as she pretended to stumble.

Her clothing fell away from her cat form even as she jumped—straight through the noose—and scrambled for the wall of the mesh enclosure they were walking past. She heard the crackle of the dog-catcher rather than feeling it through her thick fur, and realized belatedly that it must be electrified. She wasn't sure if she would have made this attempt if she'd known that, but it was far too late now, and her coat, meant for cold mountain winters, had protected her from the worst of it.

She climbed in a panic, the agility of her cat form driving her, and as the guard behind her fired and missed, and missed again as she switched directions up the enclosure and reached the roof.

She heard the zoo erupt into roars and animal cries of encouragement. A human voice even cried out, "Go, kitty cat!"

"Shit!" the guards said in unison.

More wild shots followed her. Needles hissed by as Amber made it up to the roof of the enclosure. She ran and leaped to the next. She was already two cages away while the guards were still peering up onto the first. Then she switched directions entirely and leaped across the path to a new row of cages.

Her night sight let her see better than she had as a human, and her height gave her a clear view. Lights all along the wall had come on, showing her that she had no real chance of getting over them—though she could probably squeeze between the barbed wire with little damage thanks to her coat, she was too small to make it to the top of the wall to try; nothing was built up close to it. She noticed the cameras, too, now swiveling back into the enclosure to try to find her, and had a glimpse of a helicopter on one of the low roofs towards the back.

"Goddamn it, do you see it?" one guard called to the other.

"Beehag said it was a mountain cat, not a goddamn *little* cat!" the other complained.

Their voices were clear to Amber's excellent hearing.

Instead of immediate escape, Amber looked for hiding spaces, and found one in a pile of construction materials towards the end of the zoo. While the cameras were still re-positioning to try to follow her, she dashed out of sight down the side of one of the enclosures and flattened herself to fit in a tiny space on top of a pile of rocks, under dimension lumber and roof tiles. From here, she could see a dozen more hiding places that she'd be able to make it to in short order, and she had a good vantage for seeing oncoming intruders.

She could see that the entire zoo was actually much more suited for containing big animals. She'd be able to get out, she felt, with her first taste of confidence as the adrenaline began to release its hold on her. She just had to lie low, and she'd be able to sneak out of the front gates when the timing was right.

"Call it in!" one of the guards was saying.

"Fuck no, you call it in," the other protested.

Eventually, they worked out who was making the call, and the little two-way radio crackled in return as they explained their mistake.

"Escaped?" Even over the poor quality radio from a distance, Amber recognized Alistair's voice, and it made the hackles on her neck rise.

The guards fell over each other to justify their actions,

and Amber gave a little cat smile to hear them describe her as basically supernatural.

There was a moment of silence in response, and then Alistair's crisp accent. "She won't get far. We've got her *mate* here."

Mate?

Amber knew without a doubt that they meant Tony, and it was everything she could do not to bolt from her hiding hole right then to find and defend him. But what did they mean by 'mate?' She could all but hear the emphasis that Alistair was putting on it.

The waiter at the resort had used the same word.

Whatever they meant by it, she knew that Alistair was right—knowing that they had Tony—that they might *hurt* Tony to get her, meant that Alistair had Amber as surely as if that noose *had* been tight around her neck.

Read the rest in *Tropical Tiger Spy* by Zoe Chant!